MARRIED TO A DISTINGUISHED THUG 3

SHVONNE LATRICE

About the Author

<u>Other Works by Me:</u>

Good Girls Love Thugs 1-5
Falling for a Hood King 1-4
Married to a Distinguished Thug 1-3
She's Gotta Have It 1-2
Me & My Dope Boy 1-3
Yazir & Nina 1-3
Forbidden Love with a Thug 1-3
You Needed Me 1-3
Shorty is in Love with a Real One 1-4
I Got Your Back 1-2
My Baby Is a West Coast King 1-4
Our Love Is the Realest 1-3
She Got It Bad for a Heartless Gangsta 1-4
She Got It Bad for a Heartless Gangsta: An AK Christmas
Hood Boyz Fall In Love Too 1-3
Nobody Can Love You Like Them Roughnecks Do 1-4
She Gave Her All to the Hood's Finest 1-5

Visit www.theshvonnelatrice.com for paperbacks!

facebook.com/ShvonneLatrice

twitter.com/shvonnelatrice

instagram.com/shvonnelatrice

$15.99
ISBN 978-1-966375-06-7
51599>
9 781966 375067

We'd made a lot of money tonight at Red Sugar, and it was starting to become a pattern. Every night we seemed to make more money than the previous, and anytime I was making money, I was a happy ass nigga.

I shut down my computer, and then locked all my drawers up. It was midnight and the club was still jumping, so I knew extra money would be coming in, on top of where we were at right now. A smile crept across my face at the thought.

My phone started to ring, and I saw Namiko's name flash across. "Hey pretty," I sang into the phone. I couldn't wait to go home and do some things to her sexy ass.

"Max, something bad happened to Deshawn. Get home now!" she cried and told Evelyn to calm down.

"Something bad like what?" I frowned and grabbed my jacket quickly.

"I don't know. I've been calling Kiyuki but she's not answering," she replied in a distraught tone.

"A'ight, I'm on my way," I said and hung up.

I was confused beyond belief right now at the fact that something bad had happened to my boy. *I bet it was that bitch Kiyuki's fault*, I thought for some reason. I wanted to be supportive of their relationship, but the fact that she used to try to get at me still bothered me.

I turned my office light off, and then rushed outside to the back employee parking lot.

POW!

A gunshot rang out as I pushed the unlock button on my car remote. A sharp pain shot through my shoulder blade, and I realized I was bleeding. I looked up from my wound, and couldn't believe my eyes.

POW!

Another shot pierced through my other shoulder.

POW!

A third one pierced my rib cage. My shirt was soaked in blood, and my legs collapsed under me.

"Ma! Ma! Stop!" I shouted to my mother as she stood over me with the gun pointed in my face.

"Why did you take him Max?" she sobbed as snot ran from her nose. I couldn't believe this shit, my own mother.

"Ma, don't do this. I'm your son. I'm more important than him," I pleaded with her.

"No, not anymore. All you care about is Namiko, so no, you're not more important to me anymore," she smirked and pulled the trigger once more.

Click.

Thank God the gun had run out of bullets, but I was still sitting here shot the fuck up by my own mother. I guess when they say, I brought you in this world and I can take you out; they mean it.

"Shit," my mother huffed as she attempted to pull the trigger again. *Click, click.*

"Arrgghhh," I groaned as I covered the wound in my ribcage. I doubled over in pain as my mother continuously attempted to make her empty gun shoot.

Sirens wailed as police started to head towards Red Sugar. I was thankful that someone called them, because my mother clearly didn't care to save me. No one was outside, so the person who called must've been inside of their home and heard the gunshots.

My mom ran off into the darkness and down the street, as I laid there panting heavily, praying that these ambulance muthafuckas made it to me in time.

"Sir! Sir! You're gonna be okay," an EMT yelled as he and another person helped me onto the stretcher.

"Ughhh," was all I could say, as I continued to endure the excruciating pain in my shoulders and abdomen.

"Do you know who shot you?" the police officer asked as they rushed me into the back of the ambulance.

I pretended not to hear him as they wheeled me into the truck. I didn't know what I was gonna do about my mom. I didn't wanna kill her, but I couldn't let her get away with this shit. I don't know what happened to her ass, but this wasn't cool. Son or not, I wasn't the nigga to fuck with.

After I arrived to the hospital, they placed an oxygen mask over my mouth, and I passed out a couple seconds later.

NAMIKO DAVIS

Evelyn and I sat in her car outside my house, and waited for Maximilian to arrive. It'd been about thirty damn minutes since we called to inform him about Deshawn. I'm pretty sure he could tell by my tone that this was serious, so I was confused as to why he was lollygagging.

"Where the hell is he?" Evelyn squealed, and ran her fingers through her short curly hair.

"I'm sure he will be here soon," I replied and pressed the home button on my phone to see if he'd text or called me.

"Did you tell him that it was an emergency?" she panted.

"Evelyn, you listened to the call. You heard everything I told him, relax," I shook my head. "What the hell even happened?" I added with a frown.

"I went over there to talk and-"

"Why Evelyn? He's the wrong one; he should be coming to you! I told you to stop chasing after him!" I turned my lip up.

It irritated me that she was fawning over him the way she was. He's the one who dogged her out, so if anything, he should be chasing her. Evelyn was not the type of girl to go hunting after men, so I'm not sure why she felt the need to start. If you ask me, she and Deshawn's relationship didn't appear to be that deep. I didn't see what she thought was so special about him. He seemed to be just like all her previous boyfriends. Then again, I guess it wasn't for me to understand.

"I know Nami! Let me finish!" she whimpered. "I went over there to talk, but as you can see, I had a lot to drink. He and I got into an argument after I saw that hoe of a sister you have come out of his house with a small belly. I-"

"Small belly? She's pregnant?" I yelped. I had no idea she was pregnant, but then again, Kiyuki and I weren't the best of friends at this time.

"Yes, didn't she tell you?" she quizzed.

"Hell no, she didn't. But whatever, continue," I folded my arms across my chest. Kiyuki never ceased to amaze me.

"Anyway, we argued and he tried to stop me from leaving his home drunk. He got in front of the car, and I wanted to rev my engine to scare him, but it was in drive. I'm sure you can guess what happened next," she sighed and pinched the bridge of her nose.

"I hope he is okay Evelyn," I shook my head.

I didn't want Deshawn to be dead, and I didn't want to see my best friend go to jail. They were both too young for any of this shit.

"Me too, I'm not trying to go to jail," she sniffled. "Let's go to his house and see if he's still lying there," she sat up and half smiled like that was a good idea.

"A lot of criminals get caught because they return to the scene of the crime, Ev. We're not doing that," I shook my head and chuckled lightly. Just then, my phone rung, and an unknown number flashed across.

"Hello?" I answered as Evelyn looked on intently.

"Yes, may I speak with a Mrs. Namiko Davis," a young lady replied.

"This is she."

"Hi, Mrs. Davis we have your husband down here at St. John Hospital-"

"What? What happened?" I damn near screamed. What in the entire fuck was going on tonight? First Deshawn and now Maximilian.

"He was shot three times, and he is still in emergency surgery. You can come down and wait if you'd like," she said.

"Oh, okay. I will be there," I responded before hanging up.

"What happened?" Evelyn asked with her eyes bucked.

"Maximilian was shot. Can you take me to the hospital?" I said in a low tone as I stared out the front windshield.

It seemed like I could never enjoy my marriage for more than a month or two at a time. Every time I looked up, someone was trying to mess it up, or something was happening to one of us.

"Yeah, yeah, sure," Evelyn cranked the car up, and peeled out of our roundabout driveway. I sent our nanny Dorothea a text to let her know where I'd gone.

On the way there, against my better judgment, I dialed Gwendolyn. Even though I hated her and she hated me, one thing we had in common was our love for Maximilian. She didn't answer the first time, so I decided to try once more. She didn't answer the second time, so I assumed it was just because it was so late in the night. I'm sure she would blame me for what has happened to Max.

We pulled up to St. John Hospital, and I hopped out of the car just as Evelyn was putting it in park. I couldn't wait any longer; I had to see him. I rushed inside, and damn near collided with the front desk.

"I'm here to see Maximilian Davis. I'm his wife Namiko," I ran off.

"Oh, okay Mrs. Davis. Can I just see some I.D.? And then fill out these forms please," the receptionist replied as she placed the clipboard on the counter.

Just as I was about to reach into my purse for my I.D., I realized I didn't have my purse. When Evelyn called me down, I just rushed outside; I wasn't expecting to go anywhere.

"Ma'am, I umm, I was so frantic when I heard the news that I left my wallet," I chuckled nervously.

"So you have no form of identification with you?" she raised a brow.

"No... Brionne, I read her nametag, I don't."

"I'm sorry but I can't let you in until I see some ID," she shrugged and smiled sympathetically.

"There is nothing else you could use to verify me?" I inquired and she just shook her head no.

"Ugh!" I shouted and banged on the counter. Brionne said something, but I rushed outside and bumped into Evelyn.

"Wait, why are you leaving?" Evelyn questioned.

"Because I left my fucking purse, can you please rush me back to my house?" I frowned and ran my fingers through my hair. This could not be life right now.

KIYUKI ALLEN

AN HOUR AND A HALF EARLIER...

Iheard tires screech, so I ran downstairs to the living room to wait for Deshawn to come inside. That crazy bitch Evelyn was starting to work my fucking nerves. She and Deshawn were over, yet she couldn't seem to come to grips with that. I tell you, if I didn't have this baby inside me, I would just beat her ass again.

Deshawn was taking way too long to come back inside, so I got up to go see what in the hell was taking so long. I opened the front door, and I saw a figure lying in the street next to where Evelyn was parked. Our neighbors were standing on their porch, and the wife had a phone plastered to her ear. It looked just like my baby lying in the street, but I silently prayed that it wasn't.

"Deshawn!" I shouted as I jogged over to the figure in the street. As much as I didn't want it to be him, I knew that it was.

I neared the body and it was definitely him. I dropped down next to his body, and saw he was limp. I felt for a pulse and thank God there was one.

"The ambulance is on their way," my neighbor hustled over to me, with his wife right on his heels.

"Did you see what happened?" I asked with tears sitting in my eyes.

"No honey, we just heard tires screech loudly, and we came out to see him lying there," the wife shook her head and shivered a bit due to the cold air.

Just then, the sounds of sirens blaring neared us. An ambulance and a couple of police cars sped down our street, and my male neighbor waved them down. They rushed out and began to lift Deshawn onto a stretcher.

"What the hell is going on tonight?" one of the EMT's questioned with a frown.

"Two attempted murders in one night," the other one sighed as they strapped Deshawn to the stretcher. *Nothing new in Detroit*, I thought.

"He has a pulse!" I shouted.

"Yes, we see that ma'am, and who are you?" one of them asked.

"I-I'm his wife," I lied and half smiled. "Can I ride with him?"

After looking at one another for a couple seconds, one of them replied, "Sure."

I wanted to go back inside and get my belongings, but I knew they wouldn't wait for me. I had a feeling they knew that I wasn't really his wife.

We climbed into the back of the ambulance together, and I just stared down into my baby's face the whole time. I prayed that he would wake from his concussion soon, and that this wouldn't turn into another coma.

෬

AFTER SITTING IN THE ROOM FOR ABOUT AN HOUR, THE DOCTORS had finally gotten Deshawn to wake up. I was ecstatic to see that my man was okay, but I needed more details on what happened. The doctors had questioned Deshawn themselves, but he wouldn't tell them anything, so once they left, I decided to ask him myself.

"So what happened babe?" I quizzed as I scooted my chair closer to his bed.

"Nothing Kiyuki," he sighed and laid his head back.

"I come out to you lying in the middle of the street unconscious, and you expect me to believe nothing happened? What, you just passed out?" I frowned.

"Look, be happy that I'm here right now and not dead or some shit. Damn," he turned his lip up in irritation.

"So we're keeping secrets from each other now? That's fine, I just wish you would've told me that earlier in the relationship," I scoffed and folded my arms.

"Here we go, I knew sooner than later you would get to nagging me just like Evelyn," he chuckled and shook his head.

"I'm nagging you because I want to find out what happened to you? Really Deshawn?" I raised a brow.

"That's what I said didn't I? I just told your muthafuckin' ass I ain't wanna talk about it, but you keep bumping your fucking gums!" he damn near shouted.

"Fine, fuck you, nigga. I don't give a fuck what happens to you anymore," I spat.

"Maybe you should call someone to come pick you up. I really don't want you in here with me right now," he looked over at me.

"Gladly," I replied and stood up.

Deshawn had me fucked up. I hoped he didn't think I was gonna be kissing his ass and pleading for his love like Evelyn had been. If he wanted to act stupid, he could go ahead and do so. I wasn't fucking with him until he gave me a formal apology.

As I walked down the hall and towards the exit, I saw Namiko and ugly Evelyn sitting down with their eyes closed. I wasn't gonna say anything, but I decided to not let the beef I had with Evelyn keep me from my little sister.

"Namiko, what are you doing here?" I questioned.

"Yuki, umm, Maximilian was shot. We're waiting for him to come out of surgery," she sat up and wiped the drool from the corner of her mouth.

"Shot? When? What the hell?" I plopped down in the chair across from them, and Evelyn rolled her eyes.

"Tonight, like three hours ago. I'm so frazzled," she shook her head and then took her hair down to re-do her bun. "What are you doing here?" she asked and Evelyn looked at her.

"Deshawn, I found him unconscious in the middle of our street. I'm not sure what happened, and he won't tell anybody," I replied and stared a hole through Evelyn.

"Damn, well keep me updated," she said standing up.

"Hey, I was wondering if you could give me a ride home," I smiled up at her.

"Actually, Evelyn drove me," Namiko responded and looked down at Evelyn for an answer.

"Why not?" Evelyn spat and stormed past me.

"It's fine. I will pass," I raised my brows causing Evelyn to stop in her tracks.

I was not trying to ride home with that bitch. She may try to kill my ass. Usually I would take her on, but I was pregnant now.

"How else are you gonna get home if you didn't drive?" Namiko quizzed and zipped her hoodie up.

"I will catch a taxi. See you later," I said before hopping up and storming out past Evelyn.

"Yuki!"

"It's fine Nami," I said over my shoulder.

As soon as I got home, I found my phone on the dresser, and saw I had some missed calls from Namiko, and a text from Cori. I was so tired of this bitch, and wanted so badly to tell Deshawn what she'd been doing, but I feared she actually had some info on me.

Cori: *Game time bitch.*

I powered my phone down, and then went to bed.

CORI SINEAD

THE NEXT MORNING...

I was finally back in Michigan after having a couple stupid layovers. I swear, whoever plans these plane routes needs to lay off the bottle for a while.

As I stood outside the airport waiting for my ride, I looked down at the text I'd sent to Kiyuki during one of my layovers. She didn't respond as usual, but that was okay with me. I didn't need her to say one word to accept all the turmoil I was gonna bring her way. I was getting wet just thinking about her losing in life.

A black Honda Civic pulled up, and I smiled when I saw the driver. I rushed over with my bags, and he hopped out to help me load everything into his trunk.

"Sup girl," Tyler smiled and embraced me.

Tyler was the brother of this guy named Christopher. Christopher was hired by Kiyuki and Larry to shoot at my brother and Max, causing them to crash into an eighteen-wheeler. Like typical siblings, Christopher had spilled all the tea to Tyler, and Tyler had gladly given me a few piping hot cups. I met him a couple years ago, and we fucked around for a little bit. I remembered him saying he had a brother named Christopher, who was a hood hitman. When my brother Robbie told me Deshawn and Max were looking for a nigga named

Chris who was hired to shoot them, I reached out. Because his brother ended up dead, Tyler was more than willing to help me take down the person responsible. Since Larry was already taken care of, Kiyuki was the only muthafucka left to take revenge out on.

"You look good," he smiled as he slid into the driver side of his car.

"I try," I winked and bit my lip at him. I had on some black leggings, a tight black shirt, and my hair had been freshly pressed the day I left Alabama.

"You're still pretty as ever," he nodded and took in my thick frame. Niggas who didn't even like big girls changed their minds once they saw me.

"Thanks boo. You don't look too bad yourself," I giggled like a little schoolgirl.

Tyler was an a'ight looking dude, nothing special. He had a caramel complexion, braids, and was lean. But what I liked about him was that he had a cool ass personality and was chill. I should've been after him, but I was too busy chasing Maximilian's whack ass.

"You hungry?" he asked.

"Yeah, let's get something fast though so we can go talk. I need those details because my life is depending on it," I sighed as he drove.

"Cori, baby I told you I can handle them niggas for you," he said.

"No offense Tyler, but you're no match for Max, and secondly, Deshawn is my brother. I just need to convince them that Kiyuki is a conniving hoe, and all will be well," I nodded and so did he.

After getting a chicken strip meal from Popeye's, we headed over to his apartment to eat and talk. I quickly ate my food because although hungry, I had places to be and things to do.

"So what do you have for me? You said you had something to help me convince Namiko too," I said before downing my sweet tea.

"Right, right. Well my little sister Denyse is friends with this girl named Kateria," he smirked.

"Okay? And?" I frowned. He needed to get to the fucking point. I was on edge right now. I felt like Max's people were gonna bust in any minute and blow my head open.

"Kateria was paid by Kiyuki to get some friends to jump Namiko in the parking lot of Olive Garden that day," he cheesed and so did I.

"Oh shit! It's a small fucking world!" I clapped my hands together. "So is Kateria willing to talk? Or y'all haven't gotten that far yet?" I questioned.

"Nah, we haven't gotten that far. Denyse was just telling me that Kateria was bragging to her about jumping Max Davis' wife," he responded and put honey on his biscuit.

"Good enough," I smirked. "I just need her information if you don't mind. We need to get this ball rolling," I huffed and leaned back on the couch.

Just as I did, my phone started ringing and I saw it was my mother.

"Hello?" I answered.

"Cori, you back in Michigan yet?" my mom asked frantically.

"Yeah why, what's up?" I frowned.

"Deshawn is in the hospital again. He says it's not serious, but you should go see him," she panted.

"I will see what I can do ma," I replied shaking my head. I swear Deshawn was her favorite child.

"Cori-"

"I will see what I can do, damn!" I shouted and disconnected the call.

I went into my texts, and clicked the conversation with Kiyuki's name.

Me: *Does the name Kateria ring a bell?*

MAXIMILIAN

For the third damn time, I was here in the fucking hospital. I'd never had so many injuries in such a short period of time. Deshawn wasn't able to get me out and take me to the place I'd set up like a hospital, so unfortunately this was my only option.

That however was the least of my worries. My main concern was how in the fuck my mother could shoot me; me of all people, over some no good ass nigga like Alfred. What did she expect me to do? He tried to rape my damn wife. I was so fucked up in the head right now, and nothing seemed to matter to me anymore. I couldn't care less about life right now.

"Aye bro, Namiko is back with MJ," Konz came to my room.

"All three of y'all can just go man," I waved my hand at him. He was getting on my fucking nerves.

"What? Nigga what happened to you? Ever since someone shot yo' ass, you've been acting dumb," Konz spat.

"Aye, watch who the fuck you talking to little nigga! Matter fact, get the fuck up outta my damn room before I hop off this bed and knock your little broke ass out!" I shouted.

"Word," Konz nodded and left the room quickly.

A couple seconds after he left, Namiko came into the room with our son on her hip. She looked so pretty wearing a tan dress that stopped a little above her knee. Her long hair was hanging down, and she had on sandals. My little man had on a white onesie, jeans, and white sneakers.

"Say hi to daddy," Namiko beamed and kissed his cheek. She brought him closer to me, but I just stared up at the TV as if they weren't there.

"Max, hello," she chuckled.

"Can you give me some personal space? Damn," I shook my head and exhaled heavily. I wasn't in the mood for anyone or anything.

"You don't want to hold him?" she smiled still trying to lighten the mood. That's what I loved about her, but I didn't know what to feel anymore.

I just did not like anything in my life right now. My mom really fucked me up with that bullshit she pulled. If my own mother would shoot me, then how could I trust anyone else?

"Do I look like I'm in a condition to hold anything or anyone Namiko? You're in college, act like it," I spat.

"Max what is wrong with you?" she twisted her pretty face up as she stared at me confused.

"Well let's see, I've just been shot, and contrary to popular belief, I'm not feeling too well because of it," I fake smiled.

"So now because you're shot, you get to act like a little bitch?" she raised a brow.

"Watch your fucking mouth Nami," I pointed at her.

"Or what?" she bucked her eyes as if she was wishing I said something foul.

"Can you go please? It's obvious I don't wanna be bothered right now. Damn," I ran my hands over my face.

"I'm gonna just chuck this up to you being upset about being shot. I won't count this against you," she said as she sat down in the chair.

"Nah, you can count it against me, put it in your little womanly time capsule to pull out and use later. Or whatever it is y'all do," I replied nastily.

"What's that supposed to mean?" she quizzed.

"It means do what you gotta do," I shrugged. "I really don't even give a fuck."

"Max what happened to you?" she started to tear up.

"I GOT SHOT!!!! STOP FUCKING QUESTIONING ME!" I boomed and MJ started to cry.

"We can try this again tomorrow," she said standing up. She grabbed the diaper bag, and then soothed MJ as she walked out.

"Don't bother," I called out after her but she ignored me.

I didn't know what the fuck was going on with me, but I just knew I felt weird and paranoid as fuck. I didn't want to be bothered by anyone or anything that I loved. I was so fucked up right now. The same woman that birthed and raised me, tried to kill me. The only reason she didn't is because she ran out of bullets. How fucked up is that? Everyone around me seemed to be a fraud nowadays.

"Good afternoon Mr. Davis," that nurse Melissa smiled at me.

"What's up?" I sighed.

"I see you're back to see us already," she smiled and then poked her bottom lip out as if she felt bad for me.

"I'm tired so please let me be," I said as I changed the channel on the TV. She paused for a couple seconds, and then decided to leave like I asked.

I needed to get the fuck out of here, and away from everything that I knew.

NAMIKO

The way Max behaved wasn't just a one-time thing. He was mean and nasty every time I came to see him, and I was getting worried. I assumed he would get over it but it didn't seem like he would. He was home now, and we didn't sleep in the same bed, or converse with one another. The only thing that he seemed to care about was work and our son. Whenever I would talk to him, he wouldn't respond unless it was about MJ.

I was lying in bed faced down, trying my best to go to sleep. I'd cried half the night, and I don't think my body could produce any more tears at the moment. I heard the bedroom door open, and I looked towards it to see Max wearing boxers and nothing else. I turned back around because that's how things were these days. We acted like we didn't know each other. I felt the covers being pulled off me, and I turned on my back to see him staring down at me. I didn't say anything as I watched him eye my body lustfully. He never made eye contact with me and it felt like I didn't mean anything to him anymore. He climbed into the bed, and I tried to move but he snatched me back to him. He climbed in between my legs and started to kiss my neck.

"Max stop," I whined. How dare he act like he doesn't know me 24/7, and then try to come and fuck me.

18

He ignored me and pinned my hands above my head. He was too strong for me to remove them from his grip. He kissed from my neck, to my collarbone, and then the exposed parts of my breasts. He pulled my nipple from the gown using his mouth, and began to suck hungrily. I was disgusted by his touch.

"Max get off me!" I squirmed wildly until he finally stopped sucking. He looked up at me with a hateful glare, and then rolled off me. He sat up on the edge of the bed, and dropped his head into his hands. I fixed myself, and slowly crawled up behind him. "Max talk to me baby," I rubbed his back and he moved away as if my touch repulsed him.

"I don't want to talk, I wanna fuck," he responded in a low tone. Who was he? This wasn't the man I married or fell in love with.

"Max, why are you treating me like this? What is going on?" I got off the bed and kneeled down in front of him. A smile spread across his face, and he started to caress my hair.

"I'm sorry baby. I'm just going through something," he lifted me up and put me on his lap.

"Like what? Tell me," I said.

"It's too complicated to explain," he huffed and started to remove my nightgown.

I lifted my hands in the air so that he could get it off. He threw it to the ground and then ran his strong hands all over my small frame. He laid me down on the bed, and then yanked my panties down and off. He removed his boxers, and then climbed into bed with me. He felt between my legs, and then plunged two fingers into me.

"Uhh, ahh," I slightly jumped because he was a little rough. He bit down on his lip and started to fuck me with his fingers. "Maaaxx," I cooed as he sped up. He kept eye contact with me, and then bent down to flick his tongue over my nipple. "Ugghh," I grunted softly as I released onto his fingers. He pulled them out of me and licked my juices off. He flipped me over, and then pushed my face down into the pillow. He spread my legs open, and wiggled his dick inside me from behind. It was painful because he hadn't touched me in a while.

"Shit," he mumbled as he grabbed the back of my neck to pump me hard and fast.

"Ahhh, uhhh, ahhh," I whimpered as he fucked the shit out of me.

"Fuck," he groaned as he sped up even more. He gripped a handful of my hair, and it felt like he was gonna rip it from my scalp.

"Ow Max," I whined as I grabbed the sheets and clenched my teeth.

I looked over my shoulder at him, but he gripped my hair tighter, making me face the headboard. I did not like this at all. Not because it was rough, but because he was fucking me like a hoe that he didn't care about. I'd had rough sex with him before, but it wasn't like this.

I started to dry up because I wasn't into it, and he pushed me off his dick. I fell onto my stomach and then quickly grabbed a sheet to cover my body. My vagina was sore and burning from how rough he fucked me.

"Why the fuck are you drying up?" he shouted and scowled. His sexy face looked deranged and demented.

"I'm sorry, you were just being rough," I sniffled. I wanted my husband back, not this crazy nigga lying next to me.

"Oh, now you can't take rough sex?" he smacked his lips and sat up. He walked over to his dresser with his dick swinging, and started to get dressed.

"Where are you going? It's 2am," I questioned and climbed out of the bed.

"I'm going to the party store," he responded dryly.

"You can't buy alcohol at this time of night and what do you-"

"Would you shut up? Damn! Do you ever stop nagging? All you do is nag and don't fuck me! I waited a fucking year and even married you before I could even hit, and you got the nerve to be holding out!" he growled.

"Don't fuck you? This is the first time you've even tried to touch me in weeks Maximilian. And before you got shot, we never had any problems in the bedroom!" I yelled. I was beyond offended.

He leaned down and tried to kiss my lips, but I moved my face out of the way. He was all over the place right now. Tears ran down my cheeks, and I couldn't stop them no matter how many times I wiped my face.

"What is wrong with you Max? Why have you become this person? I hate you right now, when I'm supposed to love you," I sobbed.

"I can't do this," he threw his hands up.

"Do what?" I frowned up at him.

"Us, being married to you. I'm over it," he shrugged and went to grab a duffle bag from the closet.

"Over it? So you don't love me anymore? Or what? What the hell is going on?" I screamed. I wanted to know!

"I just don't wanna be married to you. It's too stressful. I'm a twenty-five-year-old man, what do I need to be married for?" he chuckled. "I'm rich, young, and I have plenty of women to meet. No need for me to decide so young," he said nonchalantly as he packed his things.

I felt a sharp pain in my heart as I listened to him tell me all the reasons why he didn't need to be married to me anymore. I thought we were happy, but I guess I was the only one. I sat down on the bed naked, and watched my husband pack his clothes. I felt like a failure, and I was embarrassed.

"For now, I can take MJ on weekends until we get an actual custody agreement," he said as he looked around to make sure he had everything. I just nodded as tears slipped out of my eyes. I was naked as the day I was born, and I didn't even care. "Don't cry Namiko, you're gonna make someone else a happy husband. As long as he doesn't mind getting nagged and not getting any pussy," he cracked.

"Just leave Maximilian," I sniffled.

"Hey, but don't think I didn't love you, because I did at one time," he stated and then opened the bedroom door.

As soon as it closed, I buried my face into the pillow and cried the hardest I had ever cried until I fell asleep.

KIYUKI

That little text I got from Cori was driving me crazy. I hadn't been taking her as serious until she sent it. I knew if she knew Kateria, she would tell Namiko that I was behind all the shit that happened to her. Why now? Why when I was just getting a relationship back with my sister? This was the only time, in a long ass time, that I wished Larry's ass was still alive. I would have him hire someone to kill Cori. *Shit*.

"Mmmm," I cooed as Deshawn sucked on my clit. He spread my legs wider, and continued to devour me.

Ever since that little tiff we had at the hospital, he'd been trying to make up for it. He was buying me shit, eating my pussy non-stop, and taking me to really nice places.

"Ahhh," I whimpered as my body jerked. Deshawn licked me clean, and then kissed up my small belly. He dipped his tongue into my mouth, and then began to suck on my lips. "I love you," I said in between kisses.

"I love you too Yuki," he whispered back. "When do we find out what it is?" he quizzed as he palmed my belly.

"Next month we can find out," I smiled down at my stomach.

"I can't wait," he sighed and plopped down next to me.

"Deshawn, can you tell me what happened that night I found you?" I turned on my side.

"If I tell you, you have to promise to keep your mouth shut," he raised a brow at me.

"I promise," I smirked.

"Evelyn accidentally hit me with her car," he huffed.

"Accidentally? How did she *accidentally* hit you with her car?" I sat up. I knew that bitch was out of her mind.

"Because she didn't know what she was doing. She was drunk a'ight. Calm your ass down," he chuckled and checked his phone.

"And you're not gonna press charges or anything?" I quizzed.

"Hell no, for what? It's not that serious. I just told you she didn't do it on purpose Kiyuki. Let's just move on and be thankful that I'm alive," he said just as his phone buzzed.

"Who is that?" I asked.

"My sister, she's back in town and wants to see me," he replied and I almost shit myself.

"Did she say why?" I questioned.

"Nah, she just said she misses me and wants to talk," he responded and hopped up to get ready for his shower.

"Should you even be going? I mean, she set you guys up," I chuckled nervously.

"She is still my sister though. I have some questions for her. I'm hoping that she will give me some answers," he shook his head. "The last thing I wanna do is have her killed."

"But Deshawn, she tried to kill me! She shot at me for no reason!" I shouted.

"Relax Kiyuki, I'm gone address all that shit aight?" he chuckled and caressed my face. "Don't forget she possibly tried to kill me too."

"Or you could just not even go see her, and let Max finish her off," I suggested, hoping he took my advice.

"I'm going to see my sister and hear her out. That's it Kiyuki," he put his hand out to let me know that was the end of our debate.

As soon as he went into the bathroom, I pulled my phone out to call that fat bitch. I was not gonna allow her to ruin my fucking life after I'd done all that I could to stay alive. I didn't come this far to lose my life or Deshawn.

"About time you called," Cori smiled into the phone.

I peeked out the bedroom to make sure Deshawn was showering, and then sat back down on the bed before answering.

"Look bitch, I don't know what your goal is here, but I'm warning you to cut it out now. I'm not the fucking one. I thought you would've known that by now," I threatened.

She burst into laughter before saying, "No, no Kiyuki. I have the upper hand now boo. You may have schemed everyone else, but your time is up hoe."

"You honestly think your brother is gonna believe anything you have to say about me? He's in love with me, and I'm carrying his baby honey, so think again!" I spat.

"Well, he may not believe what I have to say, but that's why I'm gonna let my friend do all the talking," she laughed.

"Your friend?" I inquired.

"Yes, and he knows Christopher Brackins very well boo," she responded and my heart dropped. Chris was that nigga I fucked in order to only rat out Larry when Max and Deshawn approached him. "Hello? Kiyuki are you still there?" she asked in a fake concerned tone.

"Good luck with whatever your plan is Cori. I hope it's worth all that I will bring your way," I said and quickly hung up. "Fuck!" I yelled at the top of my lungs.

A sharp pain shot through my stomach, so I dropped back down on the bed and rubbed it. After a couple rubs, the pain subsided. I took a few deep breaths as I attempted to gather my thoughts. If Cori's little plan worked, I would be royally fucked. I would lose my sister, my man, and probably anything else that I cared about.

"Hey you okay?" Deshawn asked as he emerged from the bathroom.

"Mm hmm, I'm fine," I half smiled and sat up straight.

"I thought I heard you yell," he frowned.

"Oh, I got a little pain in my stomach," I replied and laid down flat on the bed. I suddenly got an idea that I hoped would buy me some time.

"You good?" he rushed over to me and sat on the edge of the bed.

"Not really, why don't you lay down with me?" I smiled. "Cori will understand," I added. He looked away for a couple seconds, and then climbed into the bed with me. He kissed my lips, and then my neck.

"You're such a brat," he chuckled and I cheesed.

I really needed to think of something, and fast.

MAXIMILIAN

I'd been at my loft for a couple weeks now, staying away from pretty much everyone. I only saw Namiko when I saw our son, and that was for the best. I had no interest in dealing with her. I felt like I was on a downward spiral, and she needed to be with someone who had it all together. I felt lethargic and careless, and it was nothing I could do to about it. I was trying everything in my power to care about the things that I used to love, but it was hard. I loved Namiko but I had lost my passion for the relationship.

What my mother did to me was the worst thing that could happen to someone. This was the woman I knew I could count on all my life. She was the person who loved me no matter what I did, and yet she was the same person that tried to kill me. Life didn't seem real right now, because the Gwendolyn Davis that raised me would never do the things she had done to me.

I was staying at Security Trust Lofts in downtown Detroit, and I enjoyed the peace of mind it delivered to me. I couldn't be bothered by anyone except my mother right now.

I slipped on my Karl Kani sweater, matching sweats, and some Nike slide-ins. I looked in the mirror at my rough appearance, and ran my fingers through my unkempt hair. I didn't know if I was depressed or what, but shit wasn't right; you could see it in my eyes. I grabbed my keys and phone, and headed to the door. I saw I had some missed calls from Konz, Deshawn, and a couple of hoes including Esmeralda. Namiko had finally stopped trying to change my mind about leaving her, thank God.

I pulled up to my mother's house, and took a deep breath when I saw that her car was parked outside. A tear slipped out of my eye as I stared at the front of her house. I wish I could tell people who shot me, and what had transpired, but I didn't want that hatred towards my mother. Yes, I hated her right now, but I didn't want Konz to. I didn't know what I had planned for her actually.

I fired up a blunt, and cranked my car back up so that I could listen to some music while I smoked. I bobbed my head to Kendrick Lamar's "Alright" as I took that blunt to the face. I quickly fired up another, and took that to the face as well. After feeling like I was floating on a fucking cloud, I finally exited the car.

I knocked lightly on her front door, and got no answer. I knocked a little harder this time, and still no one answered. I rang the doorbell repeatedly, and got nothing. Finally, I retrieved my key from my pocket, and let myself in. When I walked in, a putrid smell hit my nose and I almost threw up immediately.

"Ma!" I called out as I checked and made sure my gun was safely placed in my waist. "Ma!" I yelled again as I slowly walked to the back of her house.

I got to her room door, and I saw it was closed. I knocked on it lightly, and called her name again. I didn't get an answer, so I just decided to walk in.

"Ah!" I jumped back.

My mother was laid across the bed with her head blasted open. There was a gun clutched tightly in her hand, and ants were all over her body. I covered my nose with my forearm. What the fuck! I wanted to bring that nigga Alfred from the dead and kill his ass all over again. All this shit was his fault; a domino effect.

I pulled my phone from my pocket and called 911, so that they could come get my mother. I would've called the cleanup crew, but despite her actions, she deserved better than that.

Once the ambulance came and cleared everything out, I headed back downtown to Detroit Beer Co. I chose them because they were right by my loft, and I planned to get twisted as fuck. As I was downing my fifth glass of Jack Daniels, my phone rung and it was Esmeralda.

"What's up?" I answered.

"Hey you, where have you been?" she quizzed and then chuckled.

"Where I always am. What you need?" I frowned and raised my glass to the bartender to let him know to refill me.

"I need you and wanna see you. I know you have a wife, but you can come to my place," she offered.

"I ain't got a wife no more. You can come see me though. I'm not traveling for nobody that ain't my son," I replied and took a sip of my sixth drink.

"That's cool, where are you?" she asked.

"Security Lofts, downtown."

"Okay, on my way," she giggled.

"Bet," I hung up.

I dialed Namiko, because I wanted to check on my son. She didn't answer the first time, which angered me. I called again, and she picked up.

"Hello?" she answered.

"Where is Max?" I inquired.

"I just put him to bed," she responded.

"Aight. How are you?"

"Goodnight Max," she hung up in my face. I shrugged it off, and then had the bartender refill me again. I didn't care about her being upset.

By my eighth drink, I got a text from Esmeralda saying she was here. I went to my loft, and met her there. Once we got inside, I fired up my fifth blunt for the day. I wanted to be high and drunk for as long as I could be. Shit was too heavy right now.

"So what happened to your wife?" Esmeralda asked as she sat next to me on the couch. She had on some small ass jean shorts and a tube top. Damn.

"Why does it matter?" I turned my lip up and then took a pull on my blunt. I hated that females were always so interested in my damn wife, while trying to fuck me in the process.

"I'm just curious, because last time I checked you were so in love," she grinned and twirled her long hair around her finger.

"Just didn't work out," I replied and turned the TV on. I really didn't care to discuss Namiko.

"Oh, well that worked out well for me," she bit her lip and leaned closer to me.

I ashed my blunt, and then yanked her even closer. I kissed on her neck, and then pulled down her tube top to expose her perfect D cups. I took them into my hands, and sucked her nipples hungrily.

"Fuck," she mumbled and began to remove my shirt.

I stood up with her still straddling me, and carried her to the bedroom. I dropped her down on the bed, and took my sweats off as she removed her jean shorts.

"Play with yourself," I demanded.

She spread her legs wide, and began to run her fingers over her clit. I watched as she brought her fingers from her enlarged clit, and dipped them into her hole. I bit my lip, and rolled a condom down onto my dick as I watched intently.

"Uhh, ahh," she moaned as she threw her head back from pleasuring herself. "Ooooh," she released on her fingers, and then brought them to her mouth.

I climbed onto the bed, and then flipped her over onto her stomach. I lifted her ass in the air, and slid into her soaking wet pussy. I put my hand on her shoulders, and rammed into her roughly. Unlike Namiko, she didn't complain. Namiko had much better pussy however. Fuck.

"Oooh, fuck Maxxx," she whimpered as I tore her shit up.

I grabbed a handful of her hair, and wrapped it around my fist. I yanked her head back, and went in for the kill. She bit down on the pillow, as I beat her shit to a fucking pulp.

"I'm cumming, shiiiit!" she shouted and exploded all over my dick.

I smacked her fat ass, and watched as it jiggled wildly. I smacked it even harder, and smiled when I saw my hand print on her ass. I spread her ass cheeks and gripped them tightly, as I fucked her harder and faster.

"Fuck!" I called out as I filled the condom up. I hadn't had sex in the longest, so that was a heavy ass load.

I slid out of her, and stumbled to the bathroom to clean myself up. I was drunk and high off my ass. This was the only way I could get through the day. On top of what I was already going through, visions of my mother lying in bed with her brains blown out, kept invading my mind.

"That was the shit," Esmeralda bit her lip as she stood in the doorway of the bathroom.

"You're welcome," I replied dryly as I turned the shower on.

"Can I join you?" she put her hand on her hip.

"Nope," I said and closed the door in her face. For some reason, I got the feeling that fucking her was gonna be one of the biggest mistakes of my life.

DESHAWN SINEAD

Today I was finally gonna go see my sister, because I wanted to talk to her before Max found out she was back in town. I just couldn't bring myself to believe that she would set us up to have us robbed and shit. I was praying like crazy that she actually had some legit explanation as to why all these muthafuckas knew who she was, and said they were sent by her.

I kissed Kiyuki on the forehead lightly, because I didn't want to wake her up. If she got up and saw me about to leave, she would act up. For some reason, anytime I tried to leave the house, she would stomp her feet and pout. I guess it was the hormones. I had shit to handle though, so I couldn't deal with that right now.

I grabbed my keys, and then headed out to the car. I sped to the address that Cori provided me with, because I was beyond anxious to hear her out. When I arrived, I shut my engine off and took a deep breath before exiting.

"Hey bro," Cori half smiled as she stood behind the door. She looked the same, and I was happy to know she wasn't missing because she was strung out on drugs or some shit.

"What's up, whose crib is this?" I quizzed as I walked in and looked around.

"A friend's. I'm staying here until I find my own place," she replied as she closed the door behind me.

"Does Robbie know you're back? Or just me?" I raised a brow.

"Just you," she exhaled and then sat down on the couch. "Sit next to me. I miss you," she cheesed and so did I.

"So what's going on Cori? Where have you been? You've done a lot of shit baby," I frowned and patted her thigh.

"Ugh, I know what you think, but I have some crazy shit to tell you," she ran her fingers through her hair and sighed.

"Shoot," I folded my arms.

"I know that you think that I set up the robberies, and that I had Namiko jumped and shit, but it was all Kiyuki," she stared at me, anticipating a reaction.

"Kiyuki? What the fuck are you talking about?" I scowled. Cori was about to piss me off tryna pin shit on my girl.

"Deshawn, I know that while I was away y'all have become more than close, but I swear to God she was behind all that shit. She set you and Max up to be shot, and she did all that stuff to Namiko. She's also the one who had someone rob Namiko during the drops," she grabbed my hands in hers.

"Fuck off me! You lying! And to think I came over here to listen to this bullshit! How dare you try to fuck me over and then blame it on Kiyuki! I ought to knock fire from yo' ass Cori!" I shouted and snatched my hands from hers.

"Deshawn! What if I told you I had proof?" she pleaded.

"Where is the fucking proof?" I shouted.

"I know one of the girls who helped jump Namiko at Olive Garden that day! She can vouch for me!" she started to cry.

"When can this bitch vouch for you?" I raised a brow. My body was on fire on the inside right now. I felt like if I exhaled it would be flames of fire.

"I can call her right now," she said as she pulled her phone from her back pocket. "I can't believe you don't believe me," she shook her head. I didn't respond.

We both waited as the line trilled, and no one answered. Cori looked up at me, and then dialed the girl again. After what seemed like forever, she finally answered.

"Oh my gosh, Kateria, I have my brother here and I need you to tell him about Kiyuki," she begged.

"Uh, umm, yeah she paid me to have some of my friends jump Namiko," Kateria stammered over speakerphone.

"You don't sound too sure Kateria," I frowned down at Cori and she shrugged.

"No, she did," Kateria assured me.

"Would you be willing to meet up and give me all the details?" I inquired.

"Umm, yeah sure that's fine. I'm busy today though," she responded.

"Cool, meet me at the Burger King on Gratiot, across from Speedy gas station, tomorrow evening at 5:30pm. Don't be late Kateria."

"Okay," she said.

She and Cori exchanged a few more words before hanging up. I massaged my temples as I tried to process what the hell was happening right now. This shit couldn't be true. Kiyuki was my baby's mother, and I loved her ass more than anything. This situation, if true, would be so wrong in more ways than one man.

"A'ight, I'm gonna talk to you tomorrow. I will be here at 5pm to pick you up," I told Cori as I stood up.

"Okay and I have someone else I want you to meet tomorrow as well," she smirked.

"Whatever," I stormed out, and rushed to my car. I needed to speak to Kiyuki's ass ASAP.

❦

"BABE, WAKE UP," I SHOOK KIYUKI'S BODY LIGHTLY. SHE TURNED over to look at me and smiled.

"Good morning baby."

"Morning, I need to talk to you about something," I huffed.

"About what? Are you okay Deshawn?" she sat up and rubbed my back. I moved away from her touch and she frowned. "What the hell is wrong with you?" she questioned.

"Did you set your fucking sister up? Did you have her jumped, and all that other shit?" I asked and stared into her honey-colored eyes.

"Are you out of your fucking mind? Why the hell would I have my sister jumped, especially when she was pregnant at the time?" she glared at me like I was the worst nigga ever.

"I'm just asking because-"

"How could you even think I would do something like that? I thought you knew me Deshawn," she started to climb out of the bed, but I grabbed her back. She yanked her arm from me.

"Look, I'm meeting with someone tomorrow, and if they tell me some shit I don't want to hear Kiyuki, we are gonna have a problem. I love you more than anything, but all that will change at the drop of a dime if I find out you were on some sneaky shit," I told her honestly. I was trying to be strong, but I knew if this Kateria girl told me some shit I didn't like, I would be broken.

"Well, if you would believe some random person over me, then we don't need to be together anyways," she spat and then got off the bed.

"I'm just gone hear her out Yuki," I sighed.

"Hear her out for what? I already told you I ain't do that shit! I love Namiko, despite what people may think!" she yelled.

"I know you do Kiyuki, but everything is just weird as fuck right now, so just give me the benefit of the doubt," I pleaded with her.

"Fuck you Deshawn. I'm going back to my parent's home," she twisted her sexy face up and started to throw her clothes into a backpack.

"Kiyuki, don't be like that baby. I love you and you know that I'm just doing this for my sister," I said as she pulled a dress over her head.

"Then fuck and have a baby with your sister nigga," she shoved me and stormed past me out of the house.

I dropped down on the bed, and just laid back so that I could think. Life was taking a crazy turn right now.

NAMIKO

I was so over being depressed over Maximilian, but it was hard not to be. Our relationship went from sugar to shit in a matter of hours, literally. One minute we were in love and happy, he gets shot, and now he doesn't wanna be married to me anymore. Something wasn't right, but I was tired of trying to figure out what it was. Only a little ass boy would break up his family over some bullshit. Yes, it was bullshit until he told me what it was that was bothering him.

For the past few weeks, the man that I loved had become someone that he wasn't. He was angry, mean, and a womanizer. Maximilian Davis was a lot of things, but one thing I loved about him was that he wasn't a playboy. You would never see him entertaining multiple women, or being promiscuous, but lately that was something he'd become. I was starting to hear people whisper everywhere I went, about how my husband was fucking everything that had a pussy and could walk in a straight line. The only thing still keeping me in love with him was that I knew this wasn't him. Something was wrong and I just hoped he fixed it, or I could help him fix before it was too late.

I was leaving school, walking to my car when I heard someone call my name. I knew it wasn't Evelyn, because ever since she hit Deshawn, she decided to take some time off from school. It seemed like everyone was depressed these days.

"Oh hey Claudia," I half smiled as she jogged up to me. Claudia was the girl who helped rinse the coffee grounds out of my eyes, and she now worked for Maximilian as a drop girl.

"Hi Namiko, I was wondering if you had the calculus notes," she cheesed.

"Yeah I do," I replied dryly. I really didn't want to give her my shit, because I didn't know when she would give them back.

"Could I borrow them?" she asked.

"Sure, but I need them back by the next class," I said as I took my backpack off and reached inside to give her my notebook.

"Sure thing. So is Max okay?" she inquired.

"Why do you ask?"

"Oh, I just haven't seen him in a while. He sends his orders through other people," she nodded.

"Really?" I cocked my head. Maximilian's behavior was becoming more alarming by the second.

"Yes really. Well anyways, thanks for these. I will give them back Wednesday," she said and jogged away.

I quickly hopped into my car, and decided to go visit Gwendolyn, despite my better judgment... again. We hated each other, and I despised visiting her, but I wanted to know if she could shed some light on her son. She never called me back that night, but I'm sure it was because she hated me. I pulled up to her house, and I saw her car wasn't there and there was also a *for sale* sign in the yard.

As I climbed out of the car, I saw an older lady watering the grass of the house next door. I walked through the lawn slowly, until I reached Gwendolyn's door.

"Who ya looking for honey?" the older lady asked and shut off her water hose.

"Oh, my mother-in-law," I smiled.

"Is your mother-in-law Gwendolyn Davis?" she quizzed and put her hand on her hip.

"Yes, it is," I nodded.

"Well honey don't you know? Gwendolyn passed; she killed herself," she frowned in confusion at me.

"Killed herself? No, you must be mistaken," I chuckled nervously. Gwendolyn was a strong woman, and I couldn't see anything making her want to kill herself. Plus, Max would've told me.

"Ain't nobody mistaken honey. Gwendolyn blew her brains out right there in her bedroom. Her son, who I'm guessing is your husband, found her covered in ants," she shook her head in disgust.

I was in complete and utter shock right now. What in the entire fuck was going on right now? Maximilian acting weird, Gwendolyn killing herself, it was just way too much. I was hoping that I would wake up from this nightmare soon.

"I see, well thank you-"

"Janice," she smiled as if we weren't talking about death just a few seconds ago.

"Thank you Janice," I rushed back to my car and cranked it up. I knew Max was probably at his loft downtown, so I decided to pay him a visit.

⚜

"Who's there?" Max called out from behind the door. I was so nervous because I missed seeing his face. Lately he'd been picking up MJ when I was in class, so only Dorothea saw him.

"Namiko," I replied.

"Yeah?" he flung the door open.

His hair was in an afro, and shaggy looking as well as his beard. But despite all that, he was just as handsome as the day I met him. He was frowning, with his mean, fine ass.

"Can I come in?" I furrowed my brows.

"I'm kind of busy right now."

"It's important Max," I sighed.

"Is it MJ?" he asked with a worried expression.

"No he's fine, can I come in?" I cocked my head. He looked behind him, and then stepped back to let me in.

He led me to the couch, and moved a blue lingerie bra so that I could sit down. I rolled my eyes, and watched him throw it on the floor. He was wearing basketball shorts, a t-shirt, and socks. He still smelled good like always, despite his appearance.

"So what's up?" he questioned.

"Why didn't you tell me about your mother Max? Does Konz know? What happened?" I ran off.

"Nah, I ain't told nobody," he exhaled heavily.

"Babe where are the- Oh hello Namiko," that nurse Melissa stood there in one of Max's t-shirts. I ignored her and took a deep breath to calm myself. "Where are some scissors?" she finished her sentence.

"Top drawer," Max pointed to the kitchen area. I felt so disrespected. Regardless of where we were at in our relationship, this was pure disrespect.

"Max what is going on with you?" I touched his hand.

"Ain't shit going on with me Nami. I'm good," he chuckled and began to text on his phone.

"Claudia told me she hasn't seen you at Red Sugar, and I been hearing-"

"Did you come here to fucking nag me?" he growled as Melissa walked back by us to the bedroom. She had a smug look on her face, obviously entertained by Max's and my tiff.

"Goodbye Max," I said as I stood up.

"Bye, and I will be by to get MJ Friday night," he called after me but I ignored him.

Once I got into my car, tears spilled from my eyes. I stared out the window as my face became drenched. It was a silent cry, because the pain I was experiencing was too excruciating for me to make a sound.

I wasn't a hard drinker, but tonight I needed something to calm my nerves. I stopped by the party store, and bought a big ass bottle of vodka and orange juice. As I was reaching in my pocket to pay, someone slammed a twenty-dollar bill on the counter. I looked over my shoulder to see Deshawn's younger brother Robbie smiling.

"Oh hey Robbie, I got it though," I half smiled.

"I know, but I wanna pay for you," he bit his lip and then took in my appearance from head to toe.

"Thank you," I mumbled as he took his change from the clerk. I grabbed my bag from the counter, and began to walk out.

"Wait Nami, where is the party at?" Robbie chased after me and threw his hands out.

"Party? There is no party," I frowned.

"Then why the big ass bottle of liquor? I know you ain't fucking with that by yourself," he grinned.

"Well I am. Something wrong with that?" I put my hand on my hip and raised my eyebrow.

"Not at all shorty," he cheesed. "Look, I heard about ya boy, and if you need anything I'm here for you."

"You heard about my boy?" I squinted my eyes.

"Yeah, about him and his orgy parties and shit. He's living that life now," he chuckled and shrugged. "I heard it be a minimum of ten bitches every time."

"I guess," I looked down at my feet and then back up. Hearing that Max was having sex parties made my stomach churn.

"I know it's hard, but I'm here for you. Why don't you take my number down?" Robbie offered.

"Robbie, stop," I scoffed and then rushed off to my car. He called after me, but I ignored his ass.

Once I got into my car, I decided to text Maximilian.

Me: *You're having orgy parties now?*

Maximilian: *On occasions. Goodnight.*

KIYUKI ALLEN

I pulled up to my destination, and then put my car in park. I hated that I had to go back to my old ways, but sometimes life called for the scheming Kiyuki. I got out, and jogged up the apartment steps. I beat on the door with all my might, and waited for this bitch to answer.

"Oh Kiyuki, what's up girl?" Kateria smiled like I didn't know what she had been up to.

"You tell me," I said as I made my way into her apartment.

"I been good, what about you," she half smiled. I could tell she was about to shit her pants.

"I haven't been too good, because my baby daddy seems to think that I had something to do with getting my little sister jumped," I raised a brow and sat down on her couch.

"Bu-but you did," she stammered and fidgeted.

"That is not the fucking point, Kateria Johansson!" I boomed and she jumped. "Look, I don't know who the fuck you think I am, but you're about to find out real soon bitch," I smirked.

"Kiyuki, I won't say anything. I-I'll tell Cori that I can't meet up with Deshawn later today," she nodded and chuckled nervously.

"No, give me your phone," I put my hand out.

"Why-"

"Give me your fucking phone!!!" I screamed. She quickly took it from her hoodie pouch, and handed it to me. "Passcode," I said.

"It's 8854," she responded promptly.

Me: *Can't make it.*

I texted Cori.

Cori: *What? Why? I need you Kat!*

Me: *I can't lie for you, it wouldn't be right.*

"What are you doing?" Kateria asked me as she watched me type on her phone.

"Please shut up," I replied without looking at her scary ass.

Cori: *Lie? No one is asking you to lie Kateria. You told me Kiyuki had something to do with this!*

Me: *I only said that because you offered to pay me Cori, stop it.*

I'd text all that just in case Deshawn looked into Cori's phone. I then backed out of the conversation, and then pocketed her phone. I stood up to leave, and Kateria watched my every move.

"Where are you going with my phone?" she stood up as well.

"Where you're going, you won't need it," I winked and opened her front door to let my homeboys in.

"What? What is going-" she tried to say but they covered her mouth. I closed her front door so that they could do their job.

Once I got to my parent's house, I burned Kateria's phone down to ashes. I quickly showered, and then packed some outfits before needing to take a breather. This pregnancy was really tiring me out. I couldn't do the things I used to do. After I gathered my things, I sped to Deshawn's home. I let myself in, and then just relaxed.

I heard a key in the door, and a smile crept across my face. I knew it was Deshawn coming back from his 'meeting'. Once the door opened, I turned around to see my love with a disappointed look on his face. Perfect.

"So how did it go?" I quizzed with an attitude, as I stood up.

"I didn't expect to see you here," he sighed and closed the door behind him.

"I decided to give you the BOD like you asked," I said as I ran my finger along the back of the couch.

"Oh yeah? Why?" he smiled and pulled me close.

"Mmmm, I don't know," I rolled my eyes playfully. "Ah!" I giggled as he kissed on my neck.

"Cause you love me that's why," he answered for me.

"I guess," I grinned and kissed his soft lips. "So I guess you didn't hear anything bad about your baby mama," I raised a brow.

"Man, that bitch didn't even show up. I should've known Cori was lying. Talking about the girl got cold feet. Fuck kind of shit is that, this ain't no damn wedding!" he scoffed and plopped down onto the couch.

"Well, let me take your mind off of that daddy," I bit my lip and straddled him.

He kissed my neck, as he pulled my nightgown over my head. He took my hard nipples into his mouth, and devoured them gently. I threw my head back in ecstasy, as my clit began to throb.

"Shit," I whispered as he moved my panties to the side.

I pulled his shirt off over his head, as he unbuckled his jeans to release his monster. He lifted me up just a little, and then slid me down onto his long thick rod.

"Ahh, ahh," I cooed as the pain mixed with pleasure hit me.

"Damn Yuki, shit," he groaned as I bounced slowly up and down on his dick.

He took my nipple back into his mouth, and caressed my back with his hands. He squeezed my ass cheeks, as I continued to rock my hips on him.

"I swear this pussy is lethal," he commented as he scrunched up his sexy ass face.

I slipped my tongue into his mouth, as I bounced faster on him. My pelvis started to tighten, and I knew I was about to explode.

"Deshaaawwnn, ughhhh," I grunted softly as I released on him. He shot up inside me, and then rubbed my belly as we engaged in a passionate kiss.

"I love you Kiyuki Allen," he said in a low tone, in between kisses.

"I love you too Deshawn Sinead," I responded. Checkmate.

MAXIMILIAN

I needed to meet with my team, and make sure things were still in order. I'd been slacking a little bit, but I needed to get back to it. Regardless of how I felt, I needed to make money to take care of my son and his mother. Yeah my club Red Sugar and the Popeye's I owned made me money in my sleep, but I still needed to tend to my operation.

"Where are you headed?" Melissa asked, as she laid in my bed naked. There were two other girls lying next to her, but they were passed out.

"I have some meetings to attend," I replied as I fastened my chain around my neck. I really needed a haircut, but that was the least of my worries.

"I wish you could stay in bed a little longer," she giggled.

"I thought you were a fucking nurse," I spat in an irritated fashion.

"I am one, you know that," she cocked her head to the left, confused.

"How the fuck are you a nurse if you always up under me?" I asked. She hadn't left my loft in four damn days. I would leave sometimes just to get away from her.

"Because, I called in. I didn't want to spend a minute away," she climbed out the bed and switched over to me. She dropped down to her knees, and tugged on my sweats.

"Aye chill out, I have to go," I said but she ignored me. She released my dick from my boxers, and took it into her warm mouth. "Shit," I mumbled as she worked her mouth up and down my dick.

She massaged my balls, and let her saliva coat my dick. I started to hump her face, hoping to achieve my orgasm quickly. She took every stroke like a pro, which turned me on even more. I pulled out, and nutted all over her face.

"Be gone when I get back," I said before I went to the bathroom to clean myself up. I quickly washed my dick, and then left before she could protest.

※

I walked into Red Sugar, and it was quiet as hell because we weren't open. I hadn't been here in forever, and it felt weird. I shook my head and exhaled heavily as I walked to my office. When I came in, I saw my whole team, including Deshawn.

"What's up everybody?" I inquired.

"Where the hell have you been my nigga?" Deshawn frowned.

"I been umm, I been busy," I lied. Deshawn just shook his head at me and folded his arms. "So how has everything been going?" I asked the room.

"I mean it's going good, but we need you to be the boss man," Konz replied. He was now working with us.

"Fuck is you talking about man? I been the fucking boss," I scoffed. I was two seconds away from putting my foot in his ass.

"The boss of what?" Konz raised a brow. "And why the fuck is mom's house up for sale?" he added. "She ain't answering her phone or nothing!"

"A'ight umm, give me a minute alone with Deshawn and Konz please," I told everyone and they began to stand up and exit.

"You need to get your fucking shit together!" Deshawn shouted to me once everyone was gone.

"I got my shit together a'ight? You worry about your own shit!" I yelled. "And don't think I don't know that Cori is back," I added with an evil smirk.

"What exactly do you have together? You ain't been handling business, you left your family to lay up with hoes, and you been M.I.A. all around," Deshawn listed my faults.

"You don't know what the fuck is going on with me nigga!" I stood up ready to fight, and so did Deshawn. I was more than ready to whoop his ass.

"Look, y'all need to sit y'all asses down," Konz put his hands out. "Max, why the fuck is mom's house for sale?" he repeated.

"Cause she's dead! She killed herself a'ight!" I screamed.

"Nigga what? How- when did this happen?" he asked as his eyes started to water.

"Couple weeks ago," I responded dryly.

"And you didn't think to tell anyone that Ms. Gwen killed herself?" Deshawn scowled.

"Yeah, maybe I should've told Konz, but I don't owe you shit!"

"Nah, nigga you do! She was like my mother as well! You ain't the only muthafucka going through shit Maximilian," Deshawn hollered as Konz stared at the ground in disbelief. I declined to respond because he was right. "Look when you get your head together, hit me up, we got some shit to take care of," he added and then left.

It was quiet for a couple minutes, before I decided to speak up to Konz.

"Yo Konstantin, I'm sorry man but-"

"You foul as fuck Maximilian," he barked and then shot up off the couch to leave. I sat there in my office with nothing but my thoughts, until my phone started to ring.

"Hello?"

"Hey daddy, you been ignoring me!" Esmeralda whined. I knew I shouldn't have broken her off again.

"So what!" I shouted. The thought of her made my fucking skin crawl, that's how annoying she was.

"So I miss you," she giggled. "Let me come see you," she offered.

"Be at my loft tomorrow morning at 9am sharp. Be prepared to make me breakfast," I said before hanging up.

❦

WHEN I RETURNED TO MY LOFT AROUND 10PM, AFTER JOGGING around downtown, Melissa and the other girls were gone. I was happy because I needed to have time to myself. I was fucking up, and I needed to clear my fucking head.

I showered for about forty-five minutes, and then cut on Netflix to watch a movie called *Laura*. It was a film from 1944. Namiko and I loved old movies, and we always watched them together. Halfway through the movie, my mind started to drift to the time that we'd spent together. I kind of missed talking to her all night, going on dates, and definitely fucking her. What was I doing with my life? I didn't even know anymore. I didn't know if I was coming or going. Nothing at all seemed clear to me.

I picked up my phone and dialed Namiko. It rang for a little bit, and just as I was about to hang up, she answered.

"Hello?"

I was about to speak, but I just hung up the phone instead. I couldn't do it. I wasn't ready.

NAMIKO

TWO NIGHTS LATER...

„Ugh!" I slammed my pillow on its other side so that I could lie on the colder part.

As usual, I was having trouble sleeping because of my thoughts. My mind raced all night with thoughts of my family. For some reason, I just couldn't get over the fact that my life changed so quickly without any warning. I was trying to be strong and move on, but it was really hard. I was tired of putting on a mask for everyone around me. I had to smile and hold my head high, when I really wanted to curl up in a ball and cry. I had to be strong though, especially for my son.

Suddenly, I heard my bedroom door open, and I rolled my eyes.

"I'm fine Dorothea, I promise," I called out but she didn't respond. The door closed, and then I felt a hand on my back. I knew exactly who it was. "Max," I turned on my back.

He was sitting on the edge of the bed wearing a hoodie, basketball shorts, and Nikes. He just stared at me, and then ran his left hand through his unkempt hair. I sat up in the bed, and watched him. Neither one of us said anything, as he sighed dejectedly. He covered his face with his hands, and all of a sudden, his body started to jerk very lightly.

"Maximilian, what's wrong?" I peeled the covers off my lap, and scooted closer to him. No matter how bad he'd treated me, I loved him.

I pulled his hands away from his face, and then turned him to face me. His eyes were glazed, and his cheeks were soaked already. We stared into each other's eyes, as I continued to cup his face in my hands. I pecked his lips softly, and then brought his head against my chest. We laid back on the bed, and he wrapped his strong arms tightly around my petite frame. His body still jerked a little, and he was sniffling every now and then. I rubbed his back continuously, until we both drifted off to sleep in one another's embrace.

৵৵৵

THE NEXT MORNING, I WOKE UP AND HE WAS GONE. I STARTED TO get sad, until I realized the shower water was running. About ten minutes later it cut off, and then Max emerged, dripping wet with a towel around his waist. I climbed out of the bed, waiting for him to speak. After drying off, he threw on some boxers and sweats, and started to walk towards me. He sat down next to me, and then pulled me into his lap.

"Namiko, baby I know you're looking for a hell of an explanation," he exhaled. "I'm gonna tell you some things, and I need you to keep them between you and I, okay?" he looked up into my face and I nodded. "I've been feeling fucked up for the past month and a half and I felt like I was losing my mind for a little bit. I was in a place where I didn't know what was real or fake anymore. I was confused about everything in my life, and I had a sense of unhappiness."

"Why Max?" I asked as my eyes started to tear up.

"It wasn't you Nami, I promise," he said as he thumbed away the lone tear trailing my cheek. "The night that I was umm, shot, really did something to my mind frame. I had a lot of emotions, which were a mix of anger, sadness, and confusion. Just a gang of shit," he sighed and squeezed my thigh. "My mother, she umm, she's the one who shot me-"

"Ah!" I yelped and jumped back.

"Namiko, take a breather babe," he said as he adjusted me in his lap. "That whole Alfred situation was much more serious than I thought, and it kind of spiraled out of control. Anyway, that is why I pretty much became a whole new person," he finished. I was dumbfounded.

"Max, I'm so sorry. Did you kill-"

"No, no, she took her own life. I guess out of guilt, but shit, I don't know. I guess my mother wasn't who I thought she was. But the point is, baby, I owe you an apology. I shouldn't have reacted the way I did. I was cold, and most importantly, I disrespected our marriage beyond belief. I didn't handle this horrific situation the way a man, husband, and father should have and I'm sorry. You didn't deserve that. But if you'll still have me Namiko, I wanna be with you baby. I didn't mean any of the things I said about being married to you baby, I absolutely love being married to you. It was one of the best decisions I've ever made, I swear to God."

"Max, I don't know. You did some really bad things," I sobbed.

"I know and I don't expect you to just be able to pick up where we left off. I just want you to give me another chance. I don't care what I have to do; even if it's waiting another year to make love to you again, I will do it. I don't even deserve the chance that I'm asking you for, but I'm just hoping that you will still give it to me," he replied and moved my hair out of my face.

"I never wanted to be broken up, so I'm more than willing to give you a chance, but you have to really prove yourself Max. I can't be married to someone who can just wake up one day and be ready for it to be over. When I married you it was for forever, and I need to know that you see this union the same way."

"I'll prove it to you that I'm in it for the long run, watch," he smirked with his fine ass. "Fuck I missed you," he grunted and bear hugged my body as I straddled him. I wrapped my arms around his neck, and hugged him just as tight.

"I missed you too," I whispered. I was hoping that all the things that he was saying were true. I missed being with him, but getting back on my good side wasn't gonna be easy for him.

"Would you like to go to dinner with me tonight? Or is that moving too fast?" he grinned.

"I guess so," I giggled shyly.

"You better had said yes," he bit his lip and squeezed my ass roughly. He started to kiss my collarbone, and between my small breasts, as his hands caressed my back.

"Max," I nudged him.

"I'm sorry," he exhaled and stopped feeling me up. "Can I have a kiss?" he smirked.

I looked up in the air as if I was thinking, and then pressed my lips against his. He slipped his tongue into my mouth, and I let mine dance with his. His hands felt so good against my body, but I had to remind myself that he didn't deserve me in that way yet. I pulled away from him, and his eyes were still closed. I climbed off his lap, and then gathered my toiletries for a shower.

"Where you wanna go tonight?" he called after me.

"Surprise me," I winked before closing the bathroom door.

۞

I SLIPPED ON MY BURGUNDY STILETTOS THAT MATCHED MY burgundy strapless dress, brushed down my freshly pressed hair, and then covered my lips with my Tart gloss. After putting on my jewelry and my wedding ring for the first time in a long time, I was ready to go.

I walked down the hall to Baby Max's room, and saw he was sleeping in his crib. I stared down at his little chunky butt and smiled. I loved him so much, and I don't even know how I got by prior to having him. I leaned down and kissed him very lightly so that my lip-gloss wouldn't get on his freshly bathed skin.

"I love you," I whispered. I stood up straight, and then turned around to see Max standing in the doorway. He had on black slacks, a black button up with diamond cuff links, and dress shoes. He looked so handsome, especially since he'd finally gotten a haircut. "I didn't even hear you come in," I smiled.

"I know, I didn't want to disturb your little moment," he replied and squinted his eyes. We stared at one another for a couple moments, and then he stuck his hand out to lead me out.

On the way to the restaurant, we listened to Usher's *Raymond v. Raymond* album. When "There Goes My Baby" came on, Max started lip singing the words to me. He was putting his all into it, and pecking the back of my hand every now and then. I started to blush, and he laughed at me.

"Why you blushing?" he chuckled and pinched my chin.

"Cause you're stupid," I giggled as we pulled up to the Westin Hotel. We were gonna have dinner at this nice place called Roast.

We walked into the restaurant hand in hand, and we were seated immediately since we had a reservation. I couldn't lie; it felt good to be out with him again. The only problem was that I didn't feel safe in the relationship anymore. I felt like he would leave me again, and I would have no prior warning like last time.

"Good evening, can I start you off with something to drink?" the waitress smiled at Max and I.

"Can I try the Dutch Mustang," I half smiled and she nodded, before looking over at Max. He looked so good, and smelled even better. I crossed my legs to stop the flow.

"And I will have the Last Word," he told her.

"Okay, those will be out soon, and I will give you some time to look over the menu," she smiled excitedly.

"Thank you," we responded in unison.

"So how are you feeling?" I quizzed.

"I'm feeling okay. I'm still bothered obviously by the events that have transpired, but I'm taking it day by day," he shrugged.

"What made you want to come home?"

"To be honest, I missed you a lot. I thought pushing you away was what was best for me, but it was the opposite. It only made things worse, not having you around to comfort me," he shook his head.

"That's what I'm here for Maximilian. We have to communicate and be there for each other at all times. When you feel sad or depressed, I want you to come to me, not push me away until you get over it," I frowned.

"I know Nami. I know," he sighed. "And I wouldn't want you to push me away either when you're not feeling good."

"Here are the drinks, and are we ready to order?" the waitress asked.

"Yes, can I have the Dry Aged Ribeye?" I smiled and closed my menu, which she took.

"And I will take the Dry Aged NY Strip," Max handed his menu over.

"Okay, great choices. Those will be out shortly," she nodded and switched off happily.

"So how are you feeling?" Max inquired and sipped his drink.

"I'm feeling strange," I chuckled nervously, and he cocked his head to the right in confusion. "Well not strange, but very anxious."

"Why?"

"I'm just worried that you're gonna experience something else and do this all over again. It's not just me and you Max, we have a baby."

"That's understandable. And that's just gonna be part of my job to make you feel at ease about us. Neither one of us can expect you to be normal again. Shit, my fucking mother shot me, so it's gonna take time for me to be normal again too, but I just want us to deal with this process together and not apart," he stared into my eyes.

"Sounds like a plan," I cheesed.

"Give me a kiss," he said. I stood up out of my chair, and leaned over some to peck his soft lips. "I love you Mrs. Davis."

"I love you too Mr. Davis," I giggled like a little schoolgirl and sipped my drink.

CORI

I had to give it to Kiyuki because she was definitely a piece of fucking work. I don't know why I thought it would be so easy to shut her shit down, but I had a new plan in place. Kateria went missing after our little text conversation, and I'd be willing to bet my life that Kiyuki had a lot to do with that. Now my brother thinks I'm some basket case who just wants to break up his relationship. That only infuriated me further, and made me want to go harder on that stupid bitch.

I waited outside of my brother's crib with Tyler, waiting for that bitch Kiyuki to leave. So far, we'd been here five days in a row, and she never went anywhere. The only person that left the house was Deshawn, and I needed him to be at home for what I was about to tell him. I would've had Tyler at our first meeting, but he had to go out of town for something. I should've just waited, but I was anxious to end that hoe.

"Finally, damn," Tyler huffed as we watched Kiyuki switch out the house and get into her new car; courtesy of my fucking brother, I'm sure.

I hated to see that baby bump, because it would always make me feel some type of way. But then again, who was to say that it was actually my niece or nephew. I mean Kiyuki was a certified hoe, and that baby could've been anyone's.

"A'ight, let's do this shit. I got shit to do today," Tyler frowned.

"Like what nigga? You don't even have a job!" I rolled my eyes.

"And neither do you," he shot back as we exited the car.

We both ran across the street, and then up the walkway of Deshawn's home. I had never been to this house, so I guess he got it sometime after I skipped town. I was excited to see his home, but not so excited to break his heart. My brother was a good guy, and he deserved someone better than a hoe that tried to have him killed. Maybe after all this, Evelyn would take him back.

"Who is it?" Deshawn called out after I knocked on the door. I didn't say anything. "What you doing here Cori? You know it's a price on ya fuckin head," he spat.

"Just give me ten minutes, bro," I pleaded. He stared at me, and then at Tyler, before letting us in.

"Hurry up and spit it out," Deshawn folded his arms.

"Okay, Deshawn this is Tyler. Tyler is Christopher Brackin's brother," I stated.

"Why the fuck you got this nigga in my crib!" Deshawn shouted.

"Deshawn relax! Tyler is here to let you know that Chris was hired by Larry *and* Kiyuki!" I put my hand out to stop him from getting in Tyler's face.

"What? I saw the texts between Chris and Larry, and that shit didn't say nothing about my girl, a'ight." Deshawn argued.

"Look man, my brother told me that Kiyuki and Larry wanted you and Max dead because Larry got fired from the team, and Kiyuki's ego was bruised when he denied her advances," Tyler explained.

"What? Nah, you fucking lying," Deshawn shook his head frowning.

"No Deshawn, he isn't," I stared at my brother, and I could see he was overcome with all kinds of emotions.

"Nah man, not Kiyuki. She wouldn't put a hit out on me and then fuck with me on that level. Nope," he shook his head non-stop, as if he was trying to convince himself.

"Man, I ain't got no reason to lie to you. Kiyuki wanted y'all shot at, and when y'all made it out, she was tripping out," Tyler added

"Y'all gotta go," Deshawn said and opened his front door. "Right now, get the fuck out!!" he shouted.

"Deshawn I swear-"

"Get the fuck out Cori, and take this lying ass nigga with you!" he hollered.

I just dropped my head, and then walked out with Tyler right behind me. Before we even made it out of the house good, Deshawn slammed the front door. Tyler and I just kept going until we made it to the car.

"So now what you gone do?" Tyler asked as he buckled his seatbelt.

"I hope my brother comes to his senses, but for now, let's focus on convincing Namiko," I replied.

"That's gone be hard because she hates yo' ass right?" he inquired.

"She definitely does, but where is your sister at right now?" I quizzed.

"At the crib I'm sure. Why?" he raised a brow.

"I got some questions for her," I smiled and he shook his head before pulling away from the curb.

❧

WE PULLED UP TO HIS MOTHER'S HOUSE, AND I WAS HAPPY TO SEE that his sister Denyse's car was there.

"Aye ma, where is Dee?" Tyler asked his mother.

"Back," she replied dryly. Ever since Christopher was killed, she'd been very down. We walked to the back to speak with Denyse.

"What up lil sis?" Tyler smirked and leaned down to hug his little sister, who was sitting on her bed.

"Hey bro, hi Cori," she waved at me and then removed her over the ear headphones. "What y'all doing here? Have y'all heard anything about Kateria yet?" she inquired.

"Nah not yet, but Cori wanted to talk to you," Tyler responded as we both sat down on the couch in her room.

"What's up?" she half smiled.

"Is there anyone else that would be willing to come forward about jumping Namiko Davis?" I questioned.

"Umm, I think one of the chicks that helped jump her was named Dawna," she squinted her eyes as if she was thinking.

"Could you call her for us? Or give me her number?" I asked.

"I'm sure I could get her over here, but I don't know if she'd be willing to help you out. People are scared of Max, Cori," she said.

"I know, I know. But once Max find's out what Kiyuki has done, he won't even care about anybody else involved. I just need her to convince Namiko that Kiyuki was behind this," I sighed.

"Why are you trying to help Namiko? I thought you hated her for stealing Max?"

"Oh, I still hate that bitch but I'm trying to save my own ass. The only reason I've made it this long is because I heard Max has been depressed or some shit," I chuckled to mask the fact that I still cared for him.

"Alright well, let's get Dawna over here then," Denyse pulled her phone out to dial. I just hoped this shit worked, because so far it was not looking good.

"Hey Dee," Dawna answered her phone.

"What's up Dawna? I was calling because I need your help," Denyse replied.

"With what?" Dawna quizzed.

"Look, you know Kateria disappeared, so we need a new witness with the whole Namiko situation."

"Dee you know I would love to help you but, I ain't stupid. Kateria disappeared because she was snitching," Dawna said.

"So you saying you won't help?" Denyse asked with a frown, as if Dawna could see her.

"Exactly," she responded.

Fuck!

DESHAWN

I had to kick my sister out, because the shit she and that nigga were telling me was just too much to handle. I mean, it seemed like they didn't even realize how much damage they were doing by telling me this shit. Kiyuki, my baby mama, was possibly the one who tried to have me killed, robbed our clients, and then attempted to sabotage her sister. It was already enough that she tried to sleep with Maximilian in the past, but I got over that. For some reason, I saw beyond that hoe ass exterior that she showed to everyone. I knew there was something good under it, and I was right. However, the things she had possibly done were completely unforgiveable.

I poured myself a glass of Brandy, because I needed something strong right now. Shit, if I had some access to moonshine I'd take that shit to the head. The thought of my first-born being with a woman like Kiyuki was making me sick to my stomach.

I decided against texting or calling her and telling her to come home early, because I needed some time to gather my thoughts. I needed to decide on the way I was gonna approach this shit, and what side I was on. Was I gonna go with what my sister was telling me? Or was I gonna stick by my baby mama? I knew my sister like the back of my hand, but then again, I was in love with Kiyuki.

After a couple hours passed, I heard Kiyuki unlocking the front door. I stayed sitting on the couch, staring at the TV, which was turned off. I couldn't even look at her right now.

"The grocery store was so packed babe. Every line was stretched back into the aisle," she chuckled and closed the door. I ignored her and sipped my Brandy. "Are you okay?" she asked and then took the bags she had to the kitchen. "I need help with the rest of the stuff in the car, this baby has me tired," she giggled and I continued to ignore her.

"Sit down for a second," I finally replied and set my drink on the coffee table.

"What's up?" she quizzed and sat down next to me.

"Kiyuki, I need you to be honest with me. Did you have anything to do with Max and I being shot at?" I asked.

"No Deshawn. I told you that already," she whined.

"Did you have anything to do with the robberies?" I continued.

"Are you serious? How–"

"Did you!" I shouted and she jumped back.

"No, I didn't," she exhaled.

"Did you sabotage your sister and try to frame Cori?" I raised a brow and drank some more Brandy.

"No, I did not. Are we done here?" she folded her arms and rested them on her belly.

"Max is on his way over here, and we're just gonna have a little talk together with Cori," I lied and tapped her leg.

"For what!" she yelled.

"To find out the fucking truth! I can't continue this relationship with you, all the while wondering if you tried to kill me!" I hollered and stood up.

"Deshawn, don't do this. I thought you loved me?" she started to cry.

"Kiyuki I do love you, which is why I need to know the truth. If you really loved a nigga, you would be honest with me. And if you are telling me the truth, then I will apologize once I get some peace of mind, a'ight?" I half smiled and kissed her forehead.

"Deshawn, I had nothing to do with any of that shit," she responded.

"Put that on something."

"Why? That's dumb," she frowned up at me.

"Just do it Yuki. I asked Cori to do the same," I lied and stared down at her. "Put it on your parent's grave," I added. She looked up at me, and her lips trembled slightly.

"Okay Deshawn, I umm. Can you sit down? You're making me nervous," she said. I sat down and waited for her to speak. "So I was really angry and bitter, before we got close babe, and I did do some bad things. Umm, Larry and I did concoct a plan to have someone kill you and Maximilian," she swallowed a lump in her throat. I stayed quiet, waiting to hear more. I was waiting to hear something that would make me forgive her. "I was in on the robberies, a-and I set Cori up to be framed for the things I was doing to Namiko," she started to cry.

"Why Kiyuki? What the fuck?" I frowned as I felt myself tearing up as well.

"I don't know Deshawn! I was a different person then, but I'm not like that anymore baby, I promise." she sobbed and pleaded.

"I can somewhat understand the things you had done to Max and I, but to your own sister? What type of person does that shit Kiyuki?" I glared at her.

"A horrible person and it hasn't been easy harboring all of that guilt inside of me Deshawn. That's why I just decided to tell you. But now I'm different, and we have a baby coming," she smiled through the tears.

"Do we? Is that even my baby?" I searched her eyes.

"What? Yes, this is your baby! How dare you, asshole!" she screamed.

"Are you fucking serious? How dare you call me a fucking asshole when you tried to have me killed, only to turn around and start fucking with me!" I hollered and pointed into my chest.

"I didn't plan to start fucking with you Deshawn! It just happened a'ight. Don't act like I just pursued you until you couldn't deny me anymore. You came for me too!"

"So the fuck what! You did nothing to stop me! You weren't ever gon' tell me this shit, were you? If my sister never came back, you would've taken this shit to the grave hunh?" I raised a brow. She opened her mouth to talk, but just closed it back. "Exactly! This is over with Kiyuki. I will help you pack your shit, but we're done," I scoffed and shook my head.

"Deshawn no! I've changed baby, I promise! I'm not like that anymore!" she shouted as I stood up. She followed me to the back room, where I started to pack her things. "What about the baby?" she cried hysterically.

"When it gets here, we will have a test. If it's mine, we can co-parent, if we even let you live," I spat.

"I'm leaving town. You'll never see my child," she responded.

"And I will hunt you down and gut you like a fucking fish," I pointed down in her face. She jumped back and stared at me in fear.

"Please don't do this," she sniffled as I walked to the front with her shit in a duffle bag. She hit and pushed me from behind, but it didn't stop me.

"Get out," I pushed her lightly onto the porch. "You better spend all the time you can with Namiko before she finds out about this," I slammed the door in her face.

"Fuck!" I shouted and punched a hole into my wall. I rushed to my room, grabbed the engagement ring I bought, and then flushed it down the toilet. Life couldn't be any worse right now.

MAXIMILIAN

Iwalked into the house, and I smelled Namiko's toasted Ravioli. My stomach rumbled after inhaling, and I couldn't wait to throw down. I loved having a wife that could cook her ass off, even though we weren't really acting as husband and wife lately.

Namiko had been really putting me through the ringer, and honestly, I couldn't blame her. I deserted my family, which was unacceptable regardless of the situation at hand. Not only that, but I was blatantly entertaining other women right in her face, *and* talked down to her. I hated to think about what I did sometimes.

I walked into the kitchen, and saw her holding MJ on her hip while making plates. She looked so pretty wearing just a pair of jean shorts and a tube top. Her long dark hair was in a braid down her back, and I could smell her sweet perfume from where I was standing. We hadn't had sex in forever, and I was starting to become thirsty for it.

"You scared me," she smiled when she saw me in the doorway.

"My bad, what's for lunch?" I asked even though I already knew.

"Toasted Ravioli," she smirked. "Sit down and I will make you a plate," she added.

"It's two plates here. Are we having a guest?" I raised a brow.

"No, I made it for Aniku," she chuckled.

"Aniku is never here babe. She's always with *Orianna*," I used air quotes.

"You don't think she's actually with Orianna?" Namiko asked.

"Umm, no and I'm surprised that you do," I replied and leaned down to kiss MJ's cheek and then her lips.

"What is she doing then?"

"Probably with my little brother. I think they're dating," I said before sitting down at the island.

"Max, you can't let that happen, you know how your brother is!" she whined and set a plate in front of me.

"And my brother is a grown ass man Nami, I can't tell him what to do. Especially, since he calls himself not talking to me," I shook my head and bit into one of the raviolis.

"Why isn't he talking to you?" she quizzed.

"Because I didn't tell him about our mother. I can't really blame him, just like I can't blame you for not sleeping in the same bed as me," I said. She just looked away from me, and then placed MJ in his small swing sitting on the counter. "What you thinking about?" I questioned.

"Nothing," she smiled.

"You sleeping with me tonight?" I asked.

"I don't know," she replied and grabbed her plate. She picked up Max's swing, and then left the kitchen. I exhaled heavily because sexually frustrated was an understatement.

After I ate my food, I decided to drop by Deshawn's crib. I hadn't talked to him since our little argument in my office that day. He was telling me shit I needed to hear, but of course, I took it the wrong way. Plus, he hadn't been answering my calls or showing up to meetings, which was a problem.

"What's good?" Deshawn answered the door looking like his dog died.

"I'm cool. I just wanted to rap with you for a little bit," I responded. "Can I come in?" I pointed inside his house.

"Yeah," he sighed and moved out of the way for me to come in.

"So where have you been man? You been missing a lot of work, and you know you can't get paid that way," I half joked. I wasn't paying anybody who didn't put in work; I didn't care who it was.

"Oh, so you the only nigga that can disappear when he going through something?" he spat and scoffed.

"Nah, but what's going on?" I frowned in confusion.

"Man, I don't even know where to fucking start," he exhaled heavily. "Man, Larry was telling the truth when he said that Kiyuki was in on that hit put on us," he said and my head jerked back.

"Wait, what?" I furrowed my brows. I needed to hear this shit again.

"Not only did she set us up with Larry, but she was behind the robberies, and all that shit that was happening to Namiko," he stared at me and then ran his hands over his face.

"And how you find this out?" I was so fucking furious and confused. It seemed like no one could be trusted at this point. After my mom's betrayal, nothing surprised me though.

"Cori came to the house and told me. I approached Kiyuki, and after denying it for a bit, she finally broke down and told the truth."

"So she played us for real. I wonder why Chris told us Larry was the only one in on it," I said more so to myself.

"Ain't no telling what she did to convince that nigga to lie," he chuckled angrily.

"Fuck! What the hell we gone do about her? She pregnant by you, nigga. Damn!" I shouted. I wanted to wring her fucking neck.

"Same thing I said. But who knows if that baby is even mine dawg."

"True, but I'd rather us wait and find out for sure. If we kill her ass while she's pregnant, you gon' always wonder if you killed your own child," I replied.

"Yeah, you think we should kill her even after the baby gets here?" he inquired.

"What you thinking? Did she seem remorseful? Killing her would cause some problems, but so would keeping her alive. I mean Namiko may not care, but what about Aniku, and the fact that your child wouldn't have a mother," I responded.

"She did seem remorseful, but I'm just too angry to forgive her right now. I think it's because I love her ass so much. But who knows if our relationship was even real to her," he pursed his lips as if he was thinking.

"Yeah Kiyuki ain't nothing but a scheming hoe," I said and he nodded.

"Aye, but watch your mouth while she has my baby in her," he smirked and we laughed.

"Life is just unreal right now," I sighed.

"I know, how you feeling about your moms killing herself? Ms. Gwen don't even seem like the type to be that gone over a man. I know she loved Alfred, but to kill herself. That's overboard," he stood up. "You want a beer?" he asked and I nodded my head yes.

"I don't think that's why she killed herself man," I said as he walked away.

"What you mean?" he frowned as he handed me the beer and sat down next to me.

"She was the one who shot me that night," I looked at him and his mouth was on the ground. "Yeah man, I would've been dead but she ran out of bullets. I didn't realize how gone Alfred had her ass until then," I sipped my beer and stared at the magazine on the coffee table.

"Ms. Gwen shot you? Nigga you were her fucking life for as long as I can remember! This shit is wild. Between her and Kiyuki, it's hard to trust anybody out here."

"Who you telling? After that shit, everybody and everything looked foreign to me. I felt like all the decisions I made were possibly the wrong ones. From selling drugs, all the way to Namiko, I didn't know if anything I had done was right. That's why I had to get away. I went about that shit wrong though," I said.

"You did, but we all understand," he replied.

"I appreciate that, but I need Namiko to understand a little bit more than she does so I can get some pussy," I laughed and so did he.

"Man, Namiko sure knows how to shut the pussy factory down don't she?" he chuckled and sipped his beer.

"Well, let me go home so I can talk to her about her damn sister. Hopefully she will be sad enough to need some dick," I joked and we both burst into laughter.

"You the worst nigga," he cackled.

Namiko

"I can put him to bed for you Mrs. Davis," our nanny Dorothea came into the kitchen.

"Oh thanks, I need to clean the kitchen," I smiled at her as she took him from his carrier. "Goodnight chunky," I cheesed at him and kissed his fat face.

Once I cleaned the kitchen, I retired to my room, and pulled out my iPhone to dial Aniku. The thought of her being with Konz worried me a lot. Konz liked hoes, and Aniku was nothing of the sort. I knew nothing good would come from her being around him, let alone dating him.

"Heyyy Nami!" she spoke into the phone.

"When will you be home? I made chocolate chip brownies," I said to entice her.

"Ooh, can't wait to kill those. I will be back tomorrow morning though, Orianna and I are chilling," she said.

"Are you a lesbian Aniku?" I questioned.

"What? Hell no! Why did you ask me that?" I could tell she was frowning.

"Well because you spend an awful lot of time with Orianna. You sure you're not eating her pussy?" I asked to ruffle her feathers.

"What the fuck Nami?" she chuckled. "No! We're best friends and that's all," she added.

"Well when you come home tomorrow, I wanna talk to you," I said sternly.

"Fine, see you tomorrow," she sighed and then we disconnected.

"Who was that?" Maximilian asked as he entered our bedroom. I hoped he didn't think he was sleeping in here with me. For some reason it was hard for me to erase that image of that nurse bitch in his house.

"That was Aniku, saying she was over Orianna's house," I shook my head.

"Right."

"Exactly," I chuckled.

He closed the door behind him, and then walked closer to the bed. He sat down, and then moved my feet onto his lap. He started to massage them, and it felt so good.

"I wanna talk to you Nami, and I want you to just listen before you say anything or react aight?" he raised a brow. *Lord please don't let him be telling me he got that bitch pregnant*, I thought.

"O-okay," I stuttered lightly.

"So I went to see Deshawn today, and he told me some things that I need to tell you. First of all, have you spoken to your older sister?" he inquired.

"No not really. We've talked a little here there, but it's not how it used to be," I responded. I was nervous now. Even though I didn't care for my sister right now, I hoped she wasn't dead or anything.

"Alright well, I'm just gonna get straight to it. All that shit that we thought Cori was behind, was actually Kiyuki. She admitted out of her own mouth to Deshawn. She also is the one who had us shot at that time we ran into the eighteen-wheeler, and she was behind the robberies," he ran off.

"So when I got jumped that time, sh-she was behind it?" I asked, perplexed.

"Yeah baby she was. The coffee grounds, the flattening of your tires, it was all her," he rubbed my cheek.

I fidgeted for a bit, and then broke down into tears. I covered my face with my hands, and my body jerked from crying so hard. I couldn't believe Kiyuki hated me that much. How could she have me jumped knowing I was pregnant? Then on top of that, she had Maximilian and Deshawn shot at? I didn't know our problems were serious enough for her to do those things to me.

I immediately felt bad for barging in on Cori and whooping her ass the way I did. I know whose ass I wanted to whoop at the moment though. Kiyuki had it coming and I just hoped she was prepared for my wrath.

"Nami are you okay?" Max inquired as he stared into my eyes. His beautiful dark caramel skin looked so smooth, and I missed being with him in *that way*.

"What is going on Max? First your mother and now Kiyuki? Blood really doesn't mean anything," I sighed and shook my head.

"Same thing I said. Remember we have each other though," he smiled and put his hand on my exposed thigh.

He squeezed it roughly, and then made eye contact with me. His hand made its way up my leg, and then he leaned in to press his lips against mine. I slipped my tongue into his mouth, and we let our tongues wrestle with each other. He promptly positioned himself on top of me and between my legs, without breaking our kiss.

"Max," I whispered between kisses as he reached his hand under my dress to pull on my panties. "Ma-" he cut me off by kissing me roughly.

Once my panties were down, he ran his fingers over my vagina and began to play with my clit. It felt so good, and I could tell my body was missing the good sex we had. He reached under me to unzip my dress, and then released my small boobs from it. He took my nipple into his mouth, and sucked and licked it hungrily. I closed my eyes to enjoy the feeling, and that nurse walking around his loft half-naked popped into my mind.

"Move, stop," I said in a low tone and pushed his head away. He tried to stick his tongue back into my mouth, but I moved my face away. "Not yet Max," I said as I nudged him off me.

"Namiko, baby please. I'm dying here," he begged, still trying to kiss on my body.

"Just like I was dying when you left me and our son here so you could live like a single man," I spat and pulled my dress straps up.

"You got me there," he exhaled and rubbed his eyes roughly. I looked down and saw his dick was hard as a rock in his sweats. "Are you any closer to forgiving me fully?" he inquired.

"It's more so the things you said the night you left. When you told me, you didn't like being married to me. You really hurt my feelings Max, you don't get it," I started to cry as I thought about it.

"I know and I'm sorry Nami. You know I didn't mean any of that shit. I was just going through something," he replied hugging me tightly. He pulled back some and wiped my eyes with his thumb. "Can I sleep in here?" he questioned and I nodded my head yes. He pecked my lips softly, causing me to close my eyes and savor the moment.

KIYUKI

Deshawn and I were a done deal for real, and I was miserable to say the least. I've never experienced something like this ever. I've never been in a relationship that I gave two fucks about. I never understood those girls who would sit in bed and cry, while listening to break up songs by Mya, but now I got it. I was so hurt emotionally and physically, and I felt sick. Despite the shit that I've done in the past, I loved Deshawn with all my heart. Everything about our relationship was legit, at least on my end.

Now I'm looking at you with this dumb look on my face, wishing I could say I'm sorry, wishing I could make you stay. Cause I messed up I know, I was fucked up I know. Sorry ain't gonna change a damn thang. Mya's song "Sorry" blasted through my parent's home, as I sat in bed Indian style with a box of tissues. I hadn't gone anywhere or done anything in three damn days. Only thing I would do is force-feed myself in order not to starve my unborn child, and then take a hot bath. I felt so lost without my baby.

On top of what he and I were going through, I knew sooner or later, Namiko would find out what I did to her. As mean as I may have been, I cherished my relationship with my sisters, especially after losing both of our parents. I let a man come between us, and it wasn't even the man that I ended up being in love with. My life was fucked up, and I had no one to blame but myself. I prayed that things got better sooner than later, but I knew that wasn't gonna happen.

DING! DONG!

The doorbell rang, and it caught me off guard. I had no one, so I wasn't sure who would be visiting me, unless it was Aniku. I turned off the music, and then hopped off the bed hoping it was her because I missed her pretty self. When I got to the door, I looked out the peephole and saw Namiko. *Shit*, I said to myself.

"Nami, hi," I opened the door and half smiled. I didn't know what to expect from her. She didn't say anything; she just walked into the house past me. "Why didn't you use your house key?" I asked trying to get her to talk.

"Shut up Kiyuki," she stated sternly before sitting in the lazy boy. She took a deep breath and then said, "I know what you did."

"What I did?" I played dumb.

"Yes bitch, the coffee grounds, slashing my tires, ooh and most importantly, getting me jumped knowing I was pregnant," she smiled evilly.

"Nami-"

"All over a nigga? Really Kiyuki? You wanted to kill my unborn child over a man. Do you realize how fucking pathetic you are? How does your mind work?" she pointed to her head.

"Namiko, I know it sounds crazy and-"

"No, it doesn't *sound* like anything Kiyuki! It *is* fucking crazy! You let some random nigga come between us for what. We met Maximilian at the same time honey, just because you heard of him before me didn't make him yours bitch!" she yelled.

"I was in a bad place Namiko!"

"Bullshit! We've all been in bad places before, but that's no excuse to go and try to hurt the people closest to you! Despite what everyone thought and said about you, I vouched for you because you were my sister! I had your back because I loved you! Little did I know, while I was defending you, you were plotting on me! I swear I hate you right now," she flared her nostrils as her chest heaved up and down.

"And you should Nami-"

"Don't try to take the guilt trip road Kiyuki. Don't even go there with me. I will never have sympathy for your stupid ass! Only reason my foot isn't deep in your ass in this moment, is because unlike you, I have love for your baby that you didn't tell me about." she turned her lip up, "I let you hold my baby, not even knowing you tried to kill him before he could even get here," she sniffled.

"I know Namiko. I'm so sorry. Please give me a chance to repair our relationship. At least do it for mommy," I begged.

"Don't bring our mother into this Kiyuki. You weren't thinking about her when you had them girls jump me. You weren't thinking about her when you tried to have my husband killed," she spat.

"I wasn't thinking about anyone but myself," I agreed.

"Like always. And poor Deshawn, he actually left a good woman for you. Now he's stuck with you forever because of my niece or nephew," she shook her head in disgust.

"I am a good woman too! I just hit a snag!" I yelled because I was offended.

"A snag? I wouldn't exactly call it that. You're sick Kiyuki. For you to try and have someone killed, then go get pregnant by them, you have to be a terrible person," she chuckled but I knew it was an angry one.

"I didn't plan to fall in love with him. And why is everyone acting like I pursued Deshawn? He chased me, so that's his fault!" I plopped down on the couch and folded my arms.

"Yeah, well maybe if you told him that you put a hit out on him, he would've backed off," she fake smiled.

"Too late for that, we're having a baby," I raised a brow.

"You sure it's not the baby of one of the thirty other niggas you fucked?"

"Okay, you can leave Namiko. I don't need to be stressed while I'm pregnant," I stood up and walked to the door.

"Maybe you need to be jumped like me," she jabbed and got off the lazy boy.

"Yep," I replied sarcastically as she walked past me to the door.

She walked out onto the porch, and then stopped. She turned around and said, "As soon as that baby drops, I'm fucking you up."

I slammed the door in her face out of anger. This was only the beginning of the worst parts of my life.

ANIKU ALLEN

I skipped through the school parking lot, excited to go see my man. Konz and I spent every waking moment together, and I loved it. I wasn't sure how much longer he and I could date under Namiko's nose. She was getting more and more suspicious, and I was becoming more fearful.

I pulled up to Konz' condo, and smiled when I saw his car parked there. My phone was dead so I didn't get a chance to tell him that I was coming over. I was glad that I hadn't wasted my gas. I ran up the steps, and banged on his front door. I waited and waited, but no one came to answer.

BOOM!

BOOM!

BOOM!

"Konz!" I yelled from outside the door.

I was about to knock again, but the door flung open. There stood a Mexican chick with long red hair. She was wearing unbuttoned jean shorts, a bra, and nothing else.

"Konz is in the bathroom, what's up?" she cocked her head. I ignored her and barged into the condo. "Excuse me!" she called after me as she chased me through the house.

"Open this fucking door!" I screamed and banged on the bathroom door.

"Shit," I heard him mumble.

"Get out!" I yelled at the Mexican chick who was now sitting on the couch on her phone.

"Girl please. You don't want it with me," she chuckled and turned her attention back to her phone.

"Anikuuu, hey baby," Konz emerged from the bathroom shirtless, and attempted to hug me.

"Really Konz? What is she doing here? Did you tell her you had a girlfriend?" I frowned. Tears were welling up, but I used my sleeve to stop them from falling.

"Girlfriend? Since when Konz?" the Mexican chick stood up and put her hand on her hip.

"Bitch, you been knew I had a girl! Get yo ass out!" Konz shouted to her.

"I ain't tripping boo, you'll be calling me soon," she waved him off and then went to the bedroom to get her shirt and purse. "You're lucky girl, because that dick is bomb!" she clapped her hands and then strutted out.

I plopped down on the couch, and massaged my temples with my eyes closed. The tears in my eyes finally dropped and ran down my face. I felt them fall onto my knees, as my mind tried to process what just happened.

"Baby don't cry," Konz sat next to me and rubbed my back.

"Don't touch me," I gritted.

"Aniku, come on man, I messed up. Raya don't mean shit to me. She's just something to do, you know that," he said.

"Why Konz? I thought we were good. I knew I shouldn't have slept with you," I cried silently and shook my head.

"You overreacting for real Aniku. All niggas cheat every now and then baby, I just need you to work with me," he pecked my lips. "I'm not used to this shit," he added and kissed me again but more passionately.

"I thought you loved me Konz," I said in a low tone, as he kissed on my neck while unbuttoning my jean shorts.

"I do baby. I'm trying to be better, just be patient with me aight?" he stared into my eyes.

"Max isn't like you. Why can't you be like your brother?" I sniffled.

"Please, that fake ass nigga was just cheating on Namiko a couple months ago. Bitch ass was having orgy parties and everything," he spat and frowned.

"Really? I didn't even know any of this," I furrowed my brows. I'd been really neglecting my relationship with the both of my sisters for Konz' unfaithful ass. I had no idea what was going on with them.

"That's 'cause you been over here with big daddy," he bit his lip and started to pull my shorts down.

"I don't want to Konz. You just fucked that hoe," I whined as he pulled my shorts and panties to my ankles.

"I just got out of the shower," he responded as he kissed my inner thighs.

He trailed up to my vagina, and then took my clit into his mouth. He sucked on it gently, and then slipped a finger inside me.

"Mmmm," I cooed as he put one of my legs over his shoulder. "Kooonz. I hate you," I moaned as I massaged his head.

He sucked and slurped on my button, while dipping his fingers in and out of me until I came. He licked me clean as if he were a human wipe, and then dove back in. I wound my hips against his face, making him suck my clit harder. He pushed both of my legs back, and latched his mouth onto my clit, pulling the life out of me.

"Ahh, ahh, uugghh," I grunted softly as I exploded again.

He stood to his feet, and turned me over. He spread my legs, and then gently pushed my face down into the couch cushion. He lightly tapped his dick against my pussy, making me whimper like a kitten. Finally, he slipped his dick inside me and began to wound his hips into me.

"Damn Aniku," he grunted as he gripped my waist roughly. "You so fucking wet," he commented as he pumped into me. You could hear the sound of him stroking me at a medium pace.

"I'm gonna cum Konz," I cried out. That stupid bitch Baya had one thing right; Konz had some good ass dick.

"Cum baby," he said in a low tone as he sped up. He started beating it up and soon enough I was cumming like a waterfall. "Fuck," he whispered.

He slowed down for a bit, and reached around to play with my clit. As he DJ'd my button, he sped back up making my legs weaken under me.

"Ughh!" we called out together as he came and I released for the second time.

He slid his dick out of me, flipped me on my back, and then collapsed between my legs. He pulled my shirt over my head, and then began to devour my nipples. Once he got his fix, he picked his head up and sucked on my bottom lip.

"I love you aight?" he panted and I nodded with a smile.

"If I catch you again, it's over Konz," I stared into his eyes. He just stared back at me without a response.

DESHAWN

I was missing Kiyuki like crazy, but I felt guilty every time I did. I was for real in love with her snake ass, and it sickened me to think about it. To make matters worse, she was possibly carrying my baby. A part of me wanted that baby to be someone else's, but the majority of me wanted it to be mine. No matter how much I reminded myself of what she did, I still cared for her. I refused to be with her though.

"What you thinking about bro?" Cori asked as she sat in my living room.

"How crazy life is right now," I sighed and sipped my beer.

"Just be happy that you found out that bitch was a snake," my little brother Robbie commented and chuckled.

"Aye, watch your fucking mouth man," I spat.

"For what? That hoe tried to kill you and you're getting mad because I called her a bitch? Nigga grow a pair," Robbie scoffed.

"Regardless of what she did, she won't be disrespected while she's carrying my damn child. Learn some respect little nigga!" I shouted.

"Alright y'all, chill out. We shouldn't be arguing, we have enough enemies," Cori chimed in.

"Yeah, like that nigga Maximilian," Robbie smirked.

"What? How is Max the enemy?" I frowned in confusion. Robbie was always on some bullshit when it came to Max these days. It baffled me because he, Konz, Max and I grew up like brothers.

"Do you not remember he was on a mission to kill your damn sister?" he reminded me.

"Because he thought she tried to kill us and his unborn child. Now that he knows what's up, he backed off," I shrugged.

"Yeah, I heard he backed off that pretty ass wife too," he licked his lips and smiled.

"Now you need to leave that shit alone. I ain't tryna be between anymore beefs because of y'all," I exhaled and took a swig of my drink.

"You shouldn't be between shit; we're your damn siblings. Now like I said, he better not let Namiko slip through his fingers cause I'm gon' be right there to catch her fine ass," he nodded.

"I don't get the hype on her. I mean she's pretty, but she ain't all that. Y'all just like that she's half Asian," Cori rolled her eyes.

"Quit hating! That little bitch is fine as fuck. I know Max used to be knocking that shit out every night. What I wouldn't do to bang her out," Robbie replied and stared off into space.

"What does she have for me to hate on? Her B cup breasts?" Cori joked and we all chuckled lightly.

"Namiko is a beautiful girl. Cut it out," I said still laughing a little. "Plus that baby gave her a little more something, something," I added.

"Looks like I ain't the only one looking at Max's wife," Robbie raised a brow.

"I ain't looking at her like that. I just noticed her body is a little more voluptuous," I grinned and so did he.

"Speaking of voluptuous, have you spoken to Evelyn?" Robbie asked.

"Nah, I haven't," I shook my head.

"Not since she ran this nigga over like road kill," Cori taunted and laughed. I was mad I even told she and Robbie what Evelyn had done.

"Ha-ha. Shut the fuck up. Out of respect for my girl at the time, I didn't talk to her like that anyway," I responded.

"Well now that Kiyuki is a thing of the past, maybe you should get that old thing back," Robbie smiled.

"I'm straight," I replied. I had love for Evelyn, but I didn't know if I could be with her like that again.

I chilled with my brother and sister for a couple more hours before they finally left my crib. I decided to just relax and watch some movies, hopefully to keep my mind off Kiyuki. As I channel surfed, I ran across some soft porn. I was so horny that even that weak shit had me turned on. I picked up my phone to look at the time, and then quickly hopped up to leave.

I arrived at my destination, and contemplated turning back around. Then the scene of that porn popped up in my mind and I knew that I couldn't. I needed some pussy, and some guaranteed good pussy. I wasn't wasting my night on some new shit that may be whack. I wanted to slide up in something guaranteed to make me bust.

"Why are you at my house so late?" Evelyn frowned as she tightened her robe.

"That's how you welcome people to your home?" I chuckled and walked inside.

"You're not exactly welcomed. It's 11pm Deshawn, I have class in the morning," she said as she closed the door behind me.

"Hush ya mouth for a second, damn. You didn't even say hi," I turned around to face her.

"Because-"

I cut her off by slipping my tongue into her mouth. She tried to resist at first, but finally gave in to me. I pulled her robe off, and she was naked underneath. I loved that she slept naked at night. Damn, her body was the shit.

"Wait, what about Kiyuki?" she nudged me off. I guess she hadn't been in contact with Namiko lately.

"That's a done deal baby girl," I smiled and so did she.

I picked her up, and she wrapped her legs around my waist. I laid her on the bed, and then unbuckled my pants. As soon as I was naked, Evelyn sat up and took my dick into her mouth. She teased the head for a little bit, and then deep throated me.

"Go head Ev," I commented as she worked her mouth up and down my shaft.

Her mouth was wet and warm, taking me to new heights. I hadn't had any action in two weeks and I needed that shit. I humped her face slowly, and she vacuumed my shit up. My knees started to get weak because of how good she was sucking me off.

"I'm about to bust, fuck," I panted while humping her face a little faster. "Ah, fuck!" I shouted and spilled my seeds down her throat.

"Mmmm," she swallowed it up.

I pushed her back on the bed, and then climbed in between her legs. I felt between the slit, and grinned when I felt how wet she was. I reached over to her drawer, and pulled a condom out to put on. I rolled it down, and then lowered myself onto her. I kissed all over her collarbone, as I positioned the head of my dick at her opening.

"Mmmm," she bit her lip as I entered her tight hole slowly. I was kind of happy to know she hadn't been fucking other niggas. I don't know why though.

"You ain't been giving this pussy away," I nibbled on my lip as I stared down into her eyes. She shook her head no, before I dipped my tongue into her sweet mouth.

I placed her legs over my forearms, and slowly plunged into her wetness. I almost forgot how good her pussy was. I closed my eyes to enjoy the feeling, and a picture of a naked Kiyuki popped into my mind. My eyes shot open, and I immediately began to tongue Evelyn down again.

"Shit Deshawn, I missed you," she whispered.

"I missed you too," I lied. Fuck, why did it have to be a lie? Maybe I just needed to spend some time with her so we could develop what we used to have.

She draped her arms over my shoulders, and pulled me close to her. I hugged her body, and started to go ham so I could hurry up and cum.

"Ahh, ahhh," she whimpered as I pinned her legs back. Hearing the sound of my dick plowing into her wetness took me over the edge, and I busted into the condom in no time.

"You got that good shit Ev," I smirked and pecked her before rolling off her.

"You made me cum so hard," she giggled and cuddled up to me.

I tapped her to get off me so I could flush the condom and clean my dick. I returned with a warm towel for her, and then laid back down.

"So you think we can pick up where we left off?" she asked as she nuzzled up to me.

"I don't see why not," I replied as I rubbed her shoulder. I looked down into her face, and we kissed one another lightly.

MAXIMILIAN

ONE MONTH LATER...

Tonight Namiko and I were gonna resume as husband and wife, in every damn way. I felt like I suffered enough by now. I mean, how long did she want us to sleep in separate rooms and shit? I was tired of that shit, and I needed some pussy. Not only that, I missed holding her and all that lovey-dovey shit niggas liked to do.

I set the dining room up, and had plenty of roses everywhere around the room. I had a very nice gift for her and a chef here to make dinner for us. I knew she got out of class late today, so this would be perfect. She was gonna walk through that door, eat dinner with me, and then we were gonna have plenty of sex. A nigga was backed up by now.

"She's here and Baby Max is asleep," our nanny Dorothea peeked into the dining room and smiled.

"Thanks," I replied and then rushed out to the foyer. I caught Namiko just as she was going up the stairs. "Nami come here for a second," I grinned up at her. She had on a little tight ass dress, too tight to be wearing to class.

"Max I'm tired, what do you want?" she pouted and folded her arms.

"Come here," I chuckled and waved her over to me. She paused for a couple moments, and then walked over to me. "You coming in here and don't even kiss your husband," I said and then leaned down to kiss her lips.

I took her book bag from her, and led her to the dining room. As soon as we got to the doorway, her mouth dropped. She looked around the room, as I set her bag down on the floor. I walked over to one of the chairs, and pulled it out for her. She looked at me, smiled, and then sat down.

"What are you doing?" she beamed.

"Romancing your mean ass," I half joked and sat down across from her. She shook her head at me, and then grabbed one of the roses to sniff them. "I know you love white roses," I commented and she ignored me.

"Good evening," the chef I hired walked in with our plates of Lasagna, creamed spinach, and mashed potatoes.

"Thank you," Namiko smiled up at him and he nodded. He then opened some champagne, filled our glasses, and then left. We said grace and dug in.

"Thank you baby I was starved," Namiko said covering her full mouth.

"Uh yeah, I can tell. I would think you were pregnant but we know that's impossible," I taunted and she chuckled.

"I know I've been giving you a hard time, but I just didn't want to give in too easily," she replied.

"Well you've made it very hard for me baby, so good job. You make me regret leaving every day," I sipped my champagne.

"That was the plan," she laughed and I shook my head at her.

"I love your laugh, that's when you're the prettiest," I commented. "So what are you thinking about us now?" I questioned.

"I think that you have suffered long enough, and the bed has been very cold lately," she smirked seductively.

"For real?" I bucked my eyes. I wanted to make sure I was hearing her correctly.

"Yes for real," she grinned and put some more food into her mouth.

I hopped up and pulled her arm to get up with me. "Wait! Max, let's eat first!" she yelped.

"Right, my bad babe. I just got a little overwhelmed I guess," I said and she giggled. "I got something for you," I said before taking a box out of my pocket.

She put her fork down and waited for me to open it. I flipped the top up, and her jaw dropped at the sight of the chocolate diamond ring I'd gotten for her.

"Max, what did I tell you about buying me expensive gifts," she whispered as she took the box from me.

"Have I ever listened to you?" I raised a brow. "Give me your hand," I said before taking the box back. "I wanted to give you this ring as a symbol of my love for you, and to make a promise that nothing like what happened will ever occur again," I stared into her eyes and she nodded.

"I love you Max," she said in a low tone, looking pretty as hell. I couldn't take it anymore. I got up, and then scooped her up bridal style. "Max, the food!" she squealed and chuckled as I carried her out of the dining room.

"We can eat that shit later," I said and rushed up the stairs to the bedroom.

As soon as we got in, I laid her down and removed my shirt. She stood up, and then turned her back to me so that I could unzip her dress. Before it could even drop to the floor, I began to plant kisses on the nape of her neck and shoulders. I let my hands run amuck all over her small frame, until I reached her round breasts. I squeezed them gently, while still kissing her sexy shoulders. Damn, I missed fucking her. I put my hand down the front of her body, and slid it down into her panties to toy with her clit.

"Mmmm," she cooed softly.

I turned her around to face me, and leaned down to kiss her soft lips. I opened my mouth, and switched back and forth between sucking her bottom and top lip. She did the same, and then we allowed our tongues to meet. She reached down into my boxers, and began to stroke my dick with her soft hands, sending chills down my spine. I backed her into the bed, and lightly pushed her down. I dropped to my knees, and tugged her black thong down her smooth dark caramel legs. My wife was so beautiful. She stared at me with her slanted honey eyes, while biting her full bottom lip. I yanked her to the edge of the bed, and admired her center for a few moments before devouring her.

"Maaxx," she whimpered as I sucked on her clit like a lollipop.

She tasted so good, and I knew I could spend an eternity down here. I hadn't eaten pussy in months, and it was something I enjoyed. However, I wasn't about to give it to Esmeralda, Melissa, or any of them other hoes I was smacking out.

I tightened my grip on her bottom half once she started to squirm. I felt her juices spill down my chin, which only made me go harder in the paint. I took one of my arms from around her waist, and brought two fingers to her opening. I dipped them into her, and her back arched in ecstasy.

"Fuck! I love you," she cried out as I went to town on her like a buffet. I was licking, sucking, and fingering like a maniac, and it was driving her crazy. "Ahh, ahh, I'm cumming again," she shouted before her small body jerked.

I licked her clean with my tongue, and then stood up to remove my boxers. My dick sprang up, and she sat right up to take it into her mouth. She sucked it like it was the best Popsicle she'd ever had. Her eyes were closed as she enjoyed her magnificent work.

"Damn Nami," I whispered as I felt my tip bump her tonsils. She gagged very lightly, which turned me the fuck on. "Take that shit baby," I growled as she continued to go to work.

She popped her mouth off my dick, and then took my balls into her mouth. She sucked and blew on them, while using her saliva to jack me off. I'd never had a hand job this good in my life. She was licking and sucking my balls so good, I lost my damn balance and stumbled back slightly.

"Namiko fuck!" I yelled as she returned to slurp my dick like a professional. I felt my legs weaken under me, and my pelvis tighten letting me know I was about to nut. "You gotta swallow for daddy," I told her and she nodded lightly while still bobbing on my rod. "Uugghhh!" I grunted as I spilled down her throat. She took it down like a shot of smooth vodka, and then scooted to the middle of the bed.

I climbed in between her legs, and played with her soaking pussy while tonguing her down roughly. I pushed her right leg back some, and then pushed the head of my dick into her opening.

"Uhh, uuhh," she jumped modestly.

"Ahh babe," I moaned once I was all the way in. Her shit was so snug and warm; a nigga could go to sleep sucking his thumb in this shit.

I started off slowly, so that she could adjust to my size. I kissed on her neck, while groping her titties in my hands. She wasn't going nowhere for the rest of the evening. Once I felt that it was easier to pump inside her, I sped up my strokes. I pressed her legs against her body, and then dipped my tongue in her mouth as I went to town.

"Ugghh," she clenched her teeth together as I sucked on her bottom lip.

I looked to my right and kissed her inner thigh, and then sucked it roughly. I brought my lips back to hers, and kissed her passionately as she cried out in my mouth.

"I'm about to cum so hard Max," she whimpered as I started to move in a circular motion. Soon after those words left her lips, she gushed on my pole.

I picked my body up a little, and then started to slam into her pussy while pulling out very slowly. Her pretty face was twisted all up, as I kissed all over it. I grabbed her breast with one hand and hungrily sucked the nipple, and then reached my hand down to play with her clit.

"Uhhh, Ahhh, uhhh!" she screamed in a high-pitched voice.

I continued sucking her nipple, playing with her clit, and beating her shit up until we both exploded together.

"You are the fucking worst," she panted heavily as I kissed on her collarbone. "I love you, daddy," she added when I picked my head up to look into her face.

"Daddy loves you too," I smiled and so did she, before we started to kiss heavily.

NAMIKO

It felt so good to be back to normal with my husband. I was back to getting dicked down on the daily, and you could see the change in my attitude. I had more pep in my step, and I felt like I was glowing also.

It seemed like we were more obsessed with each other than before. That's what I loved about Max. No matter how long we'd been together, he never changed his ways. Most guys only do nice things until they get you, but then once they do, all the nice things stop. Not Maximilian, he was consistent and I loved it.

"Now we're all dressed up," I smiled down at my son. I kissed his fat cheeks and then scooped him up in my arms.

Since it was Friday and I had no classes, I was gonna go over to Evelyn's house. She said she had some shit to tell me, but didn't want to tell me over text or the phone. Usually when she said that, she had some juicy gossip for me. She sounded like she was finally happy and not moping over that asshole Deshawn. I buckled MJ into his car seat, and then headed over to see my best friend.

"HEY CUTIE PIE!" EVELYN BEAMED AND REACHED TO HOLD MY SON. I handed him over, and then walked inside her condo.

"Enough of that, what's this tea?" I smiled and sat down on her couch. She joined me, and adjusted MJ in her lap.

"Alright, so guess who I'm dating now?" she grinned.

"Umm, Dison?" I replied referring to an ex-boyfriend of hers.

"Dison? Bitch no! That nigga had a baby on me, I would never be back with him!" she spat and turned her lip up.

"Well I give up," I chuckled and threw my hands up.

"Deshawn bitch," she poked her lips out. I was speechless for a couple seconds, because I didn't know whether I was disappointed or angry. "Hello? Did you hear me Nami?"

"Ye-yeah, when did this happen?" I inquired.

"Like two weeks ago. He came over and basically told me he wanted to be back with me. He said that him and Kiyuki are over. I knew my baby would be back," she smacked her lips.

"Well what about the *baby* they're having?" I questioned.

"No offense but, who knows if that's even his baby. You know how your sister gets down Namiko," she scoffed.

"Yeah she is definitely a rat," I shook my head. "So you're just gonna let him come back like that?"

"I mean yeah, what's the point in making him work for it?" she raised a brow. "Everyone ain't perfect like Maximilian," she smiled.

"Max definitely isn't perfect," I huffed.

Ever since the night at the hospital, Evelyn and I hadn't really talked. She was too depressed over Deshawn, so she knew nothing about the rough patch that Max and I had. I'm sure she heard the rumors, but she wouldn't have believed anything bad about Maximilian.

"What do you mean? You have a complaint on Max. Pigs must be flying," she joked.

"Well you remember when he got shot?" I reminded her and she nodded. "Well he got really depressed, and basically told me he didn't want to be with me anymore-"

"What the fuck?" she bucked her eyes.

"Right, so at first I was trying to convince him otherwise, but I eventually gave up. He was dating all these different hoes, and I couldn't really say shit because we weren't together like that, I guess," I shrugged. "Anyway, one night he finally came to his senses and confessed that this was all because his- he got shot," I finished. I almost told her that his mother shot him, but I remembered he told me not to tell anyone.

"That is no fucking excuse! He's been injured before, that nigga just needed a reason to break it off and fuck other bitches," she twisted her face up.

"No, trust me. I know Max, and I could tell he was not himself. Getting shot really took a toll on him," I nodded. I wished I could tell her all the details so that she would understand, but I couldn't.

"Whatever, so you took his ass back?" she frowned.

"Of course I did, but I made his ass suffer first," I chuckled and so did she. "Oh and Kiyuki was behind all of that shit that we blamed Cori for. That's why she and Deshawn broke up," I added and waited for her reaction.

"Wait, even getting Max and Deshawn shot at?" she quizzed and I nodded slowly. "Please tell me that she wasn't behind you getting robbed during the drops, and jumped outside of Olive Garden?" she cocked her head and waited for my response.

"She was Ev," I pursed my lips.

"I told yo' ass that she was jealous and suspect! I hope you whooped her ass!" she shouted and I giggled.

"Oh please believe that I will, but after the baby. Unlike her, I don't want to harm that innocent child in her stomach."

"As evil as she is, the child is probably evil too. I should fuck her up myself for doing that to you," she shook her head. "What does Aniku think?" she questioned.

"Girl, I don't even see Aniku like that. She's too busy playing house with Konz, or Orianna as she would tell it," I shook my head.

"You let her fuck with Konz? Nami you know she is too sweet for that."

"I know Ev, but I feel like Kiyuki when I try to tell her not to fuck with him. I don't wanna be bossing her around, but then again, I don't want her with that nigga," I sighed.

"Try having a grown up talk with her," she suggested and I nodded.

"Evelyn if that is his baby, then what?" I asked. I knew this situation would get messy, and I was right.

Deshawn was a nice guy, but he was doing the wrong things. A part of me felt like he was using Evelyn to get over my sister, but I knew if I said that, she would go the fuck off.

"Then I'm gone be able to walk on water. That ain't his fucking baby Namiko, now stop speaking it into existence," she scowled.

"I'm not speaking shit into existence. I'm trying to get you to think realistically and logically! That nigga left you for no reason, and now that Kiyuki turned out to be a rat, he wants you back? You're better than that Evelyn," I pleaded.

"What Max did to you was no better Nami," she responded.

"There is more to our situation than what you're thinking Evelyn. I just don't want you getting played," I said.

"I know Namiko, but I know Deshawn, he would never just be with me because Kiyuki messed up. I'm pretty sure he was missing me before all these secrets came out."

"Alright Evelyn, just know that whatever happens, I got your back. I would hate to have to beat Deshawn's ass," I half joked and we burst into laughter.

"Nah, that nigga loves me. It just took him some time to realize it. We're good, I promise," she winked.

I felt so uneasy, because my gut was telling me otherwise. Max had already told me how broken up Deshawn was over this shit with Kiyuki, so I don't see how he could be over her that quick. But hey, maybe that's how guys worked. Shit, I had my own problems to think about.

KIYUKI

I was starting to do a little better, until I remembered my mortgage payment was due. Of course Deshawn had stopped paying on it like he promised, and I couldn't exactly strip in my condition. I applied to a couple jobs, but once they saw me walk in six months pregnant, I didn't get them. They would act like it wasn't a problem, but then never call me. I was broke, tired, feeling fat, and depressed. I regretted the things I did more and more each day.

It was Monday and I had a doctor's appointment for my baby. Initially I didn't want to know the sex, but now I was anxious to know what I was having. I hoped to have a boy, because I felt like a girl would grow up to be like me. I didn't want that at all for obvious reasons.

I called Deshawn to let him know I had an appointment, but he didn't answer. I just left him a voicemail, reminded him of the address of the doctor, and the appointment time so that he would hopefully show up.

I walked into the doctor's office, and to my surprise, Deshawn was already sitting here waiting. I stared at him for a bit, but he pretended not to see me. I continued to the front desk so that I could sign in and wait.

"Okay Ms. Allen, there is a fifty-dollar copay," the receptionist said.

"For what?" I frowned.

"For the appointment," she smiled. Why was she smiling? I was broke!

"I've never had to pay $50 in the past," I frowned.

"Yes, your insurance has changed and now they pay less," she smiled again but more sympathetically this time.

"Look, I don't really have $50 right now," I leaned in and whispered.

"I'm so sorry Ms. Allen, we can bill you but that is an additional $20 fee," she replied. I dropped my face into my hands for a couple seconds, until a familiar cologne hit my nose.

"Here you go ma'am," Deshawn handed two twenties and a ten to the receptionist.

"You're gonna pay for Ms. Allen?" she asked dumbly and he nodded. I looked up at him, but still he refused to look at me.

As she processed it, he went to sit back down. I got my receipt from her, and then went to sit down next to him. I looked over at him periodically, but he just stared straight ahead.

"Thank you for coming, and for paying the fee," I said but he didn't respond. "The baby is kicking, do you wanna feel," I smiled when I felt my baby move.

"I'm straight," he finally replied to me without looking. I just decided to give up on talking to him.

We waited for about twenty minutes, and neither one of us spoke to one another. The only sounds that could be heard were the receptionist talking to people, the phones ringing, and the nurse assistants coming out to call patients to the back.

"Allen?" a gray haired Hispanic guy called me.

Deshawn and I stood up and followed him to the back. He led me to the room where I would get my sonogram, and then let me know the doctor would be in shortly. Deshawn and I sat in silence, as I watched him play on his phone. I stared at different things around the room for about five minutes, before the doctor finally entered.

"Hi Kiyuki, how are you feeling?" she beamed, adding some light to the otherwise dark aura of the room.

"I'm doing okay," I half smiled.

"Well that's good. And how are you doing Deshawn? Excited to be a daddy?" she asked as she washed her hands and slid on some gloves.

"I'm doing great and yeah something like that," he responded.

"Glad to hear you guys are doing okay. Now you said you wanted to find out the sex of the baby this time right Kiyuki?" she quizzed and sat down on her stool.

"Yes ma'am," I giggled excitedly. I glanced over at Deshawn, but he was texting on his iPhone.

"Alright let's find out then," she grinned and then lifted my shirt. She spread the cold ultrasound gel on my protruding belly, and then put the machine on it. She moved it around some, as she stared at the screen. "You have a very healthy baby girl here!" she smiled.

"A girl?" I asked slightly disappointed.

"Yep, a little princess. Is that what you wanted?" she inquired.

"Oh, I didn't care what it was," I half lied. I wanted a boy, but I would love my daughter just as much.

"And Deshawn, is that what you wanted?" she asked him.

"Is there any way we could get a DNA test before the baby gets here?" he questioned catching the doctor and I off guard.

I was embarrassed and humiliated in this moment. We'd been the picture perfect couple during our last visits, but now she probably thought I was some hoe. I may have done things in the past, but this was definitely Deshawn's baby.

"I, umm, well yes we can. I must warn you though that it is quite pricey," she responded and I could tell she was still somewhat baffled by his request.

"How much would it cost me? And how soon can this be done?" he quizzed.

She looked from him to me, and then back at him before speaking. "It's about $1000. We can take the samples now, and you can write a check if you'd like," she smiled uncomfortably.

"Let's do it please," he fake smiled and nodded.

She looked back at me and I just cheesed. Once she cleaned off my stomach, we went and had samples collected for the prenatal DNA test. Once it was done, Deshawn wrote her a check and we headed out.

"Deshawn, you know she's yours," I said once we made it outside.

"All I know is that you're a scheming, conniving ass hoe. I ain't taking care of no baby until I get proof that it's mine. I'm pretty sure it ain't though," he smirked.

"I will let the test speak for itself. I can't wait to see the egg on your face when it comes back that you're the father," I shook my head and tugged on my door handle.

"You do that," he spat and then hopped in his car quickly.

I shook my head, and then pulled out my phone. I was hungry as fuck, and I wanted to see how much money I had in my account. I opened the Wells Fargo app, and saw I only had $100 to my name. I exhaled heavily, and then took myself to Walmart to buy a little bit of groceries.

KONSTANTIN "KONZ" DAVIS

❦

"Fuck Konz," this girl named Tiona called out as I pounded her from the back. A smile crept across my face as I watched her ass jiggle.

"Arrggh," I growled as I filled up the condom.

After I caught my breath, I slid out of her. I shook my head as I eased the condom off my dick. I needed to hurry up and shower before Aniku got out of class. I needed to get her out of here too.

"What you got planned for the rest of the day?" Tiona asked.

"Not sure yet, but I know I have to go meet with my brother in twenty," I lied.

"Damn for real? I was hoping we could go to dinner," she smiled with her sexy ass.

"Nah baby, I got some shit to do. Aye, but I'm about to shower real quick, so you should head out," I said as I sat up and got out of the bed.

"Fine, but you better call me tonight!" she pointed her finger in my face as I slipped up my boxers.

"A'ight, I'll see what I can do," I grinned and then led her to the door after she got dressed.

"Bye boo," she winked and then kissed my cheek. I watched her ass as she walked to her car, and then closed the door.

I know what you're thinking, and yes, I do love Aniku, but I love pussy too. What am I supposed to do when she's in class all day? The only time I'm occupied is when Max gives me work to do, which hasn't been much. I've been ignoring his ass for keeping my mom's death a secret for so long, so he hasn't had a chance to put me to work. By saying that when I'm laid up in the crib, I think about getting pussy.

I hopped into the shower, and thoroughly washed my body. I didn't want any of Tiona's scent to be on me when Aniku came over. I knew she wasn't gon' leave me, but I didn't wanna hurt my baby.

I was putting deodorant on, when I heard Aniku banging on the front door. I rushed to the front, opened it, and she ran into my arms. I grabbed her face and slipped my tongue into her mouth.

"I missed you," she bit her lip and smiled.

"I missed you too baby. You looking good today," I bit my lip as I eyed her little body. Her smooth chocolate skin was glistening, and looking gorgeous as ever.

"Thank you," she giggled and pushed her long curly hair behind her ears.

Even though I'd just gotten some pussy, there was nothing better than fucking Aniku. I was the only one to ever fuck, and that made it all the better.

"Let's go eat," she said.

"I wanna eat something else first," I pulled her close and began to kiss her passionately.

I kissed her and backed her to my bedroom, and then all the way to the bed. I pulled her shirt off over her head, and then pushed her onto the bed. I bent down to unbuckle her jeans, and then yanked them down. She laid back on the bed, and then hopped back up.

"What the fuck is this?" she frowned and held up Tiona's earring. *Shit*.

"Oh, that must be my homeboy's girlfriend's earring," I lied and tried to grab it from her, but she pulled away.

"Why would it be in *your* bed?" she asked as her eyes began to water.

"Because, I let him use my bed! Give me the fucking earring Aniku!" I shouted and snatched it from her.

"I'm done," she said and then stood up to pull her jeans back up.

"Done? Done with what?" I quizzed angrily.

"Done with you! I told you if you cheated on me one more time I was leaving you, so this is it!" she cried and put her shirt back on.

"I didn't cheat on you. I told you that earring was my boy's girl," I reiterated. She wasn't going no fucking where. I'll be damned if she was gon' be out here fucking other niggas.

"How dumb do you think I am Konstantin?" she frowned and sniffled. I didn't speak quickly enough, so she stormed past me and through the living room.

"Where the fuck are you going? I told you I didn't cheat! You not about to be fucking other niggas!" I hollered.

"I'm gone do whatever the hell I wanna do, just like you. If I meet someone else then I'm just gone be with them," she folded her arms across her chest and smirked.

"Baby, I swear I've been faithful. I don't know how that earring got there. I let my boy Ashton use my bed with his girl, and maybe that's what it is," I said in a nicer tone.

"You swear?" she raised a brow.

"I swear baby, you know I love you," I grinned and pecked her full lips.

"Alright Konz. Let's go eat though, we can do it when we get back," she cheesed.

"That's cool."

Aniku and I decided to go have lunch at T.G.I. Fridays, and I was actually happy because I was hungry. We didn't wait too long since it was the middle of the week, which was a plus.

"What you getting?" she asked.

"I for real want some ribs, you?" I quizzed as I looked over the menu.

"I want a steak," she replied.

"I thought you had to work Konz?" I heard a voice say. I looked up and saw Tiona standing there with a hand on her hip. "Who is this bitch?" she pointed to Aniku.

"Aye chill out T, this is my girlfriend Aniku," I said standing up. Aniku looked between Tiona and me, and I could tell that she was furious.

"Girlfriend? Since when? You didn't think to tell me you had a girlfriend when we were fucking earlier?" Tiona spat.

"Lower yo' fucking voice!" I shouted in a whisper. I looked at Aniku, and she was resting her back with her arms folded. "Ain't nobody fucked you!" I turned back to Tiona.

"Whatever nigga. Girl, don't believe anything he says. We've been fucking for weeks," Tiona giggled and switched off.

I made sure she was far away, and then I slid back into my seat across from Aniku. She just stared at the menu like nothing had happened.

"She's lying baby," I said and waited for her response.

"Oh, is that why she has the other earring matching the one I found in your bed?" she raised a brow. I just opened and closed my mouth repeatedly. "Exactly," she nodded and returned her attention back to the menu.

Aniku didn't talk to me for the rest of the meal, and as soon as we got to my house, she left.

Me: *How long you gone be mad baby?*

Aniku: *It's over Konz, goodbye.*

Me: *What? Nah! Let me talk to you!*

I waited and waited with no response from her. I called her phone about six times, and she didn't answer once. For the first time in my life, I was actually worried about something.

DESHAWN

I was lying in Evelyn's bed, inhaling the scent of the breakfast she was making me. I didn't know what to do with myself, but I needed to get my shit together. I was laid up with Evelyn every damn night, telling her things she wanted to hear but I didn't mean. I felt like the worst nigga right now.

"It's ready," Evelyn stood in the doorway and flashed her beautiful smile.

I smiled back and then peeled the covers off me. I followed her to the kitchen, and sat down in front of the plate she made me.

"Damn waffles, and a breakfast scramble? You weren't playing," I laughed and picked up my fork.

"Yeah, I wanted to feed my man. You've been living without my cooking for a while," she replied. "So are we like officially together?" she raised a brow and ate a waffle slice.

I exhaled heavily, and then sipped my orange juice. "Evelyn, I'm having a lot of fun with you right now, but I'm not trying to be in nothing too serious. I mean I went from you straight to Kiyuki and I need some time first," I explained and waited for her response.

"I get it. You're not messing around with anybody else though right?" she quizzed.

"Nah, you know it's only you and me," I smirked and she nodded.

After we ate breakfast, I showered, brushed my teeth, and got dressed to leave. Today was the day that Kiyuki and I found out if the baby was mine. My gut was telling me that it wasn't, and I was actually nervous to hear the truth. At least I could cut all ties with her after this.

"Good luck," Evelyn rubbed my back.

I sped to the doctor's office, and just tried to understand my thoughts. Why did I want this baby to be mine? I should've been praying every night for it to be some other nigga's baby, but I wasn't. I didn't pray for it be someone else's because I was scared that God would grant my wish. I turned up the heat in my car, because the cold air was starting to make sick. I arrived at the doctor's office in no time, and took a deep breath before getting out. *It's not yours Deshawn, be happy*, I told myself.

"Hello," Kiyuki waved to me as I sat a seat away from her in the waiting area.

She looked so pretty in the dress that she had on. I never knew what people meant when they said people had a pregnancy glow until now. Her long hair was in a slick ponytail, and her honey-colored eyes were so bright. I quickly broke my stare.

"Sup," I replied dryly. She turned away from me and caressed her belly.

We waited in silence, for what seemed like an eternity, and then finally the guy called us to the back. He led us to her doctor's office, and we sat down next to one another. I looked over at her out the corner of my eye, and she had her eyes closed rubbing her stomach. It was so crazy that we went from being over the moon in love, to barely speaking, but it was all her fucking fault.

"Hello Deshawn, Kiyuki," the doctor walked in with a folder. "How are you guys?" she grinned.

"Good," we both said in unison.

"Okay, here are the results. Who wants to open them?" she asked and looked back and forth between Kiyuki and I. Kiyuki pointed to me, so she handed me the envelope.

"Ahem," I cleared my throat as I opened the envelope slowly. I knew I would be a little devastated by the results, but it was best I find out now. *Quit being a bitch*, I thought.

I damn near ripped the shit open after my miniature pep talk, and scanned it frantically with my eyes. I was 99.9% the fucking father. I folded it back up, and then glanced over at Kiyuki who refused to look at me.

"Well?" the doctor inquired.

"I'm the dad," I smiled and showed her the paper. I kept looking over at my baby's mother, and I could see how angry she was.

We talked with the doctor for a little while, and then headed out to the parking lot. No words were spoken between us, but I had some things to say to her.

"Look Yuki, I'm gonna start back paying on the mortgage and all the other bills you're struggling with okay?" I said.

"I don't need it anymore. I got a job," she replied and stuck the key into her car door.

"You do need it, and I'm not gonna have you stressing about bills while carrying my baby," I grabbed her arm lightly, which she snatched.

"See you at the next appointment," she spat before getting into her car. I watched her speed out of the parking lot.

⁂

"How did it go?" my sister Cori asked as soon as I walked into her new apartment.

I didn't want to see Evelyn at the moment, or be by myself. Max was out with Namiko and his son, so my sibling was the only person available.

"I don't really know how to answer that," I responded and sighed. I sat down on her couch and put my face into my hands.

"I'm so sorry bro, but I told you it wasn't yours," she smacked her lips and shook her head. "It's annoying to me that she tried to play you like that! If I never would've exposed that bitch, you would be thinking that baby was yours," she ran off.

"It is mine Cori," I picked my face up out of my palms. Her jaw was damn near on the floor as she stared at me in disbelief.

"Are you sure Deshawn?" she frowned.

"I am positive. We had a test taken by the doctor, so it's not like she went and got it done herself and manipulated it," I replied and stood up to go get a beer from her fridge.

"So what now?" she asked once I returned.

"I'm gone take care of my baby, fuck you mean?" I furrowed my brows. What kind of fucking question was that?

"No, I mean aren't you back with Evelyn? How is she gonna feel knowing that Kiyuki is having your baby for sure?"

"First of all, Evelyn and I are just friends a'ight? And if she loves me like she says she does, she will accept my daughter," I said before sipping my beer.

"I have a feeling none of this will be that easy. But what I do know is, you better not try to be some happy family with Kiyuki. That bitch is bad news," Cori glared at me, and I nodded as I took a swig of my beer. Lord have mercy.

MAXIMILIAN

My brother and I hadn't spoken to each other on a personal level in a little over a month. I know I was wrong for withholding our mother's death, but it wasn't intentional. I was in another place in my life, and I wasn't thinking about the right things to do.

"Don't leave us," Namiko pouted as she and my son laid in bed.

"As adorable as you both are, I have to go. I will be back by nine though," I smiled and kissed her lips. She cupped my face so that we could kiss a couple more times.

"Tell daddy to stay," she said to MJ, and picked him so that he was facing me. He just stared at me, drooling on his chubby hand. "You are no help," Namiko said to him before kissing his face.

"Cause he knows his dad has shit to handle," I smirked and slipped on my Jordan 11's.

"And where is that?" Namiko quizzed.

"Hopefully to make amends with my little brother. He's still angry with me about that situation with my mother," I responded.

"He must really be mad, because Aniku isn't going over there every night like she used to. In fact, she hasn't been over there at all for the past two weeks," she said.

"I know you're happy."

"It's bittersweet because she's sad," she pursed her lips.

I finished dressing, and then jogged down to my car. I tried calling Konz to make sure he would be at home, but of course, he ignored my call. I sped out of my driveway, and headed over anyway. I pulled up twenty minutes later, and was relieved to see his car sitting outside. I quickly got out, treaded up his walkway, and banged on the door.

"Aye, quit banging on my shit!" he yelled from behind the door. I shook my head at him and waited patiently. I heard him look through the peephole and smack his lips.

"What's good?" he answered holding the door open.

"I just wanted to talk for a little bit," I replied before walking in. He showed a disgusted expression, but I didn't give a fuck. I sat down on his couch, and waited for him to take a seat as well. "Look man, I'm sorry about the way I handled moms. Some shit popped off between she and I, and I was dealing with a lot," I said.

"Explain," he responded dryly.

"A'ight, so the night in the parking lot of Red Sugar when I got shot, it was by moms," I glanced over at him and he just stared at the wall.

"Ma wouldn't do no shit like that!" he shouted.

"Why would I lie Konz? I loved her just as much as you did. I wished like hell that she wasn't the one behind that gun but she was! Why do you think I became so fucked up in the head after it happened?" I frowned.

"Man, what did you do to her?" he teared up.

"You know Alfred and I had some beef, and shit just got out of hand," I explained the best that I could. I really didn't like discussing murdering people with anybody, even if it was my brother.

"Why couldn't you just let her live? You was always in her fucking business," he grimaced. I wanted to knock his ass upside the head.

"What? I did let her live her fucking life, to an extent! That nigga was using her and you know it! Alfred disrespected my fucking wife, and me and he paid for it. Simple as that!" I yelled.

"This is so fucked up right now," he said as he ran his hand over his fade.

"It is fucked up, which is why I want us to be close again Konz. Life is too short, and it's too many disloyal muthafuckas out here for brothers to be fighting," I said.

"I hear you. I just wish Ma didn't go out like that. It was so fucking selfish of her to take her own damn life like that!" he scoffed.

"I agree, but I want you to remember her for who she was to us the majority of her life. The times when she was with Pops, not the woman Alfred turned her into," I said.

"I'll do my best, but it's gone take time," he shook his head.

"Who you telling? I still think about her trying to kill me every day. It's hard for me to understand how she went from who she was to who she became," I said more so to myself.

"On a somewhat lighter note, I think I want some advice," he chuckled.

"You think you want some advice, or you do?" I smiled.

"A'ight I do. But I don't know if I'm actually gon' take that shit, just to let you know," he responded and I waited for him to talk. "So I'm pretty sure y'all know, but if not, Aniku is my girl; well she was. She don't wanna be with me no more, because she caught me cheating on her ... twice," he looked over at me.

"And you wanna know how to get her back or what?" I quizzed.

"Yeah man, I been calling her and texting her constantly and that don't work. Then I left her alone for a couple days and that didn't do anything, so what should I do?" he questioned.

"I thought I'd never see the day that you would have woman problems. What happened to only smashing hoes?" I laughed.

"C'mon Max, I need this advice," he smacked my arm.

"A'ight, a'ight. You gon' have to dig deep to find that romantic bone, and pull out all the stops. But, only go get her back if you gon' do right Konz. Aniku is a sweet girl and she deserves better than that."

"I know but it's hard. How do you just be with one woman?" he frowned.

"You have to be scared of losing her, and have the ultimate respect for her. If you respect your woman, you don't even want to give other women the satisfaction of being able to say they fucked you. Same goes with you being scared to lose her. If you know you don't ever wanna feel the way you're feeling right now, it'll stop you from sticking your dick in anything but her. And lastly, if you love her, hurting her is the last thing you'd wanna do," I explained and he nodded.

"That's how you feel about Nami?" he questioned.

"Yeah, I love her more than anything and I love being with her. It's never a dull moment, like we're actually homies," I replied.

"Namiko as a homie? I can't imagine it," he cackled.

"Well imagine it. She's one of the best homies too," I nodded.

I chopped it up with my brother for a little bit longer, and then decided to pay someone else a visit. I was passing out apologies like no other. I felt like I was on tour for apologies, like damn!

I pulled up to Cori's crib after Deshawn texted me the new address. I hoped she would accept it, but I couldn't worry about that too much. She would either take what I had to say and move on, or continue to be angry. It was up to her.

"Max?" she answered the door with a confused expression.

"Hey Cori, can I come in? I won't be long," I half smiled and she blushed.

"Ye-yeah of course Max," she grinned and let me in. "It seems like forever since I've seen you," she chuckled lightly.

"Yeah, it has been. I just wanted to apologize for accusing you of all that shit that was happening to my wife," I got straight to the point.

"It's cool. I know it looked bad on my end, and you were just trying to protect her," she replied.

"Yeah, I'm glad you understand and I hope we can be cordial," I smiled at her.

"I don't see why not," she giggled. After a couple moments of silence, she asked, "Are you happy?"

"You mean in general? Or with my wife?" I tried to clarify.

"Both I guess, but I'm more so interested in finding out if you're happy in your marriage. I heard you guys had a rough patch," she said.

"Yeah, I'm happy in general and very happy with my wife. That snag wasn't anything major," I responded standing up to leave. This conversation was headed in a direction I didn't want it to.

"That's good. You leaving already?" she quizzed with a frown.

"I am, but it was nice talking to you," I sighed and stretched.

"See you later Maximilian," she licked her lips and stood behind the door.

"Peace out baby girl," I said before kissing her cheek lightly.

She pulled me into a hug, and held me tightly. I didn't move, and just let her savor the moment. After a few moments, she pulled back and stared into my eyes. She caressed my face, and then let me go. I walked down to my car, happy that this damn apology tour was over.

NAMIKO

I adjusted Baby Max on my hip, as I walked out of Starbucks. I had a long day, and all I wanted to do was go home and relax. I hoped Maximilian was at home, because I wanted to lay up under my man.

"We meet again," I turned around to see Deshawn's brother Robbie. I hated running into him, but it was bound to happen occasionally.

"Oh, hey Robbie," I said sipping my iced coffee.

"You look beautiful today, where are you headed?" he quizzed and adjusted his snapback.

"Oh, I've been at school all day. I just wanted to get some fresh air with my baby," I smiled at MJ and kissed his face.

"I see. How is everything on the home front?" he questioned.

"It's great. I'm really happy," I cleared my throat. "But I have to cook and do some studying, so I will see you around Robbie," I said.

"Still can't get that number?" he called after me.

"Not while I'm still married," I flashed my ring over my shoulder, and power walked to my car.

Robbie was annoying as hell. I think he was only pursuing me because he had this unspoken beef with Maximilian. If he thought he was gonna get at me as some type of revenge, he was sadly mistaken.

When I got home, I put Baby Max in his playpen to tire him out, and then started on dinner. Unfortunately, Maximilian wasn't home, so I couldn't lay up with him and eat. While the pork chops were in the oven, I went to check on Aniku. All she'd been doing lately was going to class, and coming home to her room. She would eat her food in there and everything.

"Hey, you doing okay?" I asked as I walked into her room. She was lying across the bed in her pajamas already.

"Yeah I'm good," she responded dryly.

"I see you haven't been to Orianna's lately," I chuckled and sat on her bed.

"Yeah, we had an argument," she sighed and then looked up at me. "Are you cooking tonight?"

"Yes, I'm making baked honey glazed pork chops, broccoli, and scalloped potatoes," I answered.

"Ooh good."

"Aniku what's wrong? I know you were going to see Konz and not Orianna, and now you're not going to see him anymore. So what's up?" I quizzed.

"Konz is just a friend, and I wasn't going to see him. I was actually at Orianna's," she continued to lie.

"Aniku Allen, don't lie to me. I'm not gonna beat you up or anything, tell me the truth," I nudged her and she half smiled.

"Konz is... Konz is my boyfriend. Well he was my boyfriend until about three weeks ago," she exhaled heavily.

"What happened?" I inquired.

"I don't want to tell you because I'm pretty sure you already know," she huffed.

"You caught him with another girl," I stated. She just nodded and tears began to fall from her eyes.

"I caught him twice Nami," she sobbed hysterically.

"Shhh, calm down Aniku. It's okay. Just move on now that you know he can't be faithful to you," I rubbed her back and hugged her tightly.

"I can't just leave him, I love him," she cried. "You don't understand because Max is perfect," she sniffled. "It's hard loving someone who isn't perfect."

"Aniku, nobody is perfect. Look we haven't talked much, so you don't really know what has been going on. Max and I broke up, a couple months ago if you can call it that. Right after he got shot, he told me he didn't want to be married to me," I said and she stared in disbelief. "While we were on this little break or whatever, he was sleeping with other women. I was just as hurt as you but I had to keep my head high for my baby. So you see; I do know what it's like to love someone who isn't perfect, Aniku. You just have to decide whether or not their imperfections are something you can accept."

"I'm sorry, I didn't know that Nami. I guess I was too caught up with Konstantin," she wiped her nose. "So you think I should take him back?" she quizzed.

"Only if he's sorry and you think he won't do it again. Otherwise, you're a beautiful young girl and can have any man you want. It's not like you have kids with him," I smiled and rubbed her cheek.

"Nami, I lost my virginity to him," she whispered. It felt like my heart had stopped as I processed what she'd just told me.

"Why Aniku?" I frowned in confusion.

"Because I thought we were in love, and that he would be my husband anyway. Now I'm thinking that it was a bad idea," she explained.

"Aniku, what about your promise to mom and dad? How could you let him get in your head like that?"

"It wasn't all him Nami, I wanted to do it with him. It's hard to resist that when you're in love," she half smiled. "I'm not a hoe I swear," she added and I chuckled.

"I know you're not a hoe Aniku," I sighed. "I just wished you waited."

"Sometimes I feel that way too, but it's too late," she shrugged.

"It is, but at least you can move on to someone who will treat you better. But if you think Konz is the one, I won't stop you," I threw my hands up.

"He has to be the one," she yelped.

"Why?" I furrowed my brows.

"Because I-I'm pregnant Nami," she replied.

Suddenly it felt like the room was spinning, and that I was gonna throw up. I felt like it was my fault for not stepping in and saying something about her friendship with Konz from the beginning. She was only in college, how was she gonna have a baby? And did Konz even love her? Ugh, I felt sick.

"Nami? Did you hear me?" she teared up.

"Aniku, I-I just don't know what to say I guess. You know just because you're pregnant that doesn't mean he has to be with you right?"

"Yeah I know. I wanna keep my baby though," she giggled. "I can't wait to dress it up."

"Aniku, a baby is way more work than playing dress up. You can't live your life the way you want when you become a mother. Everything you do will affect that baby directly. Times like now when you want to stay in your room and cry. You can't do that because your baby will need you to function no matter how shitty you feel," I shook my head at her stupidity. Konz and Aniku as parents was probably the worst combo in history.

"I know," was all she said before picking up her phone to text. I was hoping I woke up and that this would be a fucking nightmare.

KIYUKI

I'd finally gotten a job working at the front desk of an AAA branch. Surprisingly they didn't mind that I was pregnant. I was only making $16.40 an hour, but it was better than having no income at all. My shift was 8:30am to 4:45pm, and sometimes it was hard to wake up in the morning, but I was slowly getting used to it.

I walked into the house after stopping to get a burger from Wendy's. I was so tired and hungry. I tried to eat healthy, but after my salads, I would end up just stuffing my face with some pizza or something anyway. Hopefully since I was only twenty-four, my body wouldn't take too much work to get back to normal.

As soon as I finished my burger, I heard the doorbell ring. I was scared of who it was, because pretty much everyone I knew hated my guts. I hoped that they at least spared my life until my daughter was born. She didn't deserve to die because of my old ways.

"Who is it?" I called out as I stood out of the way of the door. I didn't want them to shoot me through the door.

"Deshawn, open this shit up, it's cold!" he barked.

"What do you want?" I questioned still contemplating on whether or not I should let him in. This could all be a set up.

"I wanna check on you! Open the door Kiyuki!" he yelled.

I ran to the side window so that I could see if anyone was with him. I looked out and saw him standing at the door alone. He looked so good wearing an all-black Jordan jogger suit. I saw him exhale heavily as he waited for me to open up. I walked around to the door, and checked myself in the living room mirror to make sure I didn't look too bad.

"Finally! What, you got a nigga up in here?" he frowned and looked around the living room as he walked in.

"I was making sure you weren't coming over here to kill me or something." I replied and locked the door.

"Why the fuck would I kill you when my baby is still in you?" he turned his lip up at me in disgust.

"Whatever Deshawn, what are you here for?" I folded my arms across my chest.

"What are those D cups now?" he chuckled and gestured towards my breast. I was usually a B-cup, but this pregnancy had definitely gotten me into the C's.

"I'm sleepy and I need a bath, so what do you want?" I repeated.

"I wanted to see how my baby was doing. I wanted to make sure you were eating right, and all that good shit," he said as he plopped down on my couch.

"Yes she's fine. I will call you if anything changes, now can you leave please?" I raised a brow and stood over him. He reached up and caressed my stomach, making me jump a little. "How much longer?" he questioned.

"Just two more months," I smiled down at my belly and rubbed it.

"Cool. Sit down man, I don't like people standing over me," he smirked up at me. I sat down next to him, and stared straight ahead. I then grabbed my pop off the coffee table, and started downing it. "How are you getting money Yuki?" he asked.

"I have a job." I replied dryly.

"Where at? It bet not be no hoe shit you doing," he spat.

"If you're gonna insult me you can leave," I started to tear up. I hated being pregnant in times like these. Sometimes I would even cry on commercials that weren't even sad.

"Why are you crying?" he quizzed in a low tone, and then thumbed my tear away. I moved my face away from his fingers, and continued to stare straight ahead.

"I'm fine, move," I nudged him back.

He grabbed my chin and turned me to look at him. He pressed his lips against mine, and when I tried to pull back, he wouldn't let me. He slipped his tongue into my mouth, and began to suck on my lips. He ran his big hand over my belly, and then started to tug on my maternity work pants.

"No, Deshawn stop," I pulled my face away.

"Why?" he furrowed his brows. "You already have someone new?"

"No, but you do. I know you ran right back to Evelyn, Deshawn. Have you forgotten that we pretty much know all the same people?" I raised a brow.

He moved off me, and sighed. He took a deep breath, and then leaned forward, putting his elbows on his knees. I watched him massage his temples, as I picked my pop back up to polish it off.

"I still love you," he whispered to himself. A smile crept across my face, only because he couldn't see me. "And I don't want to," he added. I didn't say anything at all. He finally looked over at me, and stared into my eyes. "Why did you have to do the shit you did Yuki? None of the beefs you had with any of us were that deep for you to go so far," he frowned.

"I know Deshawn. I was in a bad place. I told you that. All of my life I've been the type to get what I wanted or schemed to get what I wanted because I felt like no one cared about me. If no one cared about me, then why should I care about them?" I shrugged. "But when we started hanging out, it changed me. I saw that no one cared about me because I wasn't someone that made it easy to be cared about. No matter how horrible I was at first, you still kept chipping away at me because you knew it was something better under, and that's why I fell in love with you Deshawn," I said as a tear slipped out of my eye. "I'm so tired of being angry and hating people. I've been doing it since I was fifteen-years-old, and I'm tired of it," I sniffled. "Now here I am, broke, alone, fat, and depressed," I added.

"You're not fat, you're beautiful," he rubbed my back.

"Thank you," I chuckled and then sniffled again.

He pushed my hair behind my ear, and then leaned over to kiss my neck. He then covered my mouth with his, and gently pulled my pants down. He pulled my shirt over my head, and then leaned down to kiss my stomach repeatedly. He pulled my panties down, and then threw them onto the floor. After he stood up, he scooped me up and carried me to my bedroom. Once he laid me down, he began to undress himself as I watched.

"I missed you," he said in a low tone as he climbed in bed and got on top of me. He dipped his tongue into my mouth, and then positioned his dick at my opening. I hadn't been touched in forever, so I tensed up upon entrance. "Oooh shit," he whispered.

"I missed you too," I finally admitted once he was inside me.

"Am I hurting the baby?" he stopped pumping me and I shook my head no.

He continued to go in and out of me slowly, while sucking my lips. I missed having sex with him so much. He kissed me harder, as he started to go in a circular motion.

"I love you Kiyuki," he said into my mouth as our tongues wrestled.

ANIKU

Konz hadn't let up, and honestly, he was starting to break me down. I loved his ass even though he was such a fuck up. On top of that, I found out I was pregnant by him, which wrecked my sister. I knew it would which is why I didn't want to tell her, but it wasn't something I could've hidden forever.

After I put on a yellow dress, I slipped into my sandals. I slicked my edges down, and then grabbed my purse. I was finally gonna go see Konz' begging ass tonight, and I wanted to tell him the news. Hopefully he would still want to work it out, knowing I was pregnant.

"Hey baby," Konz smiled looking just as sexy as ever. His hair was freshly cut, and his brown skin was blemish free like always.

"Hi," I responded dryly. He shook his head and laughed before closing the door.

"I'm glad you finally decided to come and see me baby girl," he plopped down on the couch, and then patted the cushion next to him so that I could follow suit. I sat down, but nice and far away, "Damn, you don't wanna sit next to daddy?" he frowned.

"Nope," I said putting extra emphasis on the P.

"Well anyway, I called you over here because I wanna be back with you," he shrugged and stared at me.

"That's all you have to say?" I turned my lip up.

"Aniku, I said everything else in the texts I sent you. Didn't you say I sounded like a broken record?" he had a confused expression.

"So what! I finally come over and all your crusty ass can say is that you wanna be back with me? I'm leaving," I stood up.

"Okay, okay Aniku wait," he grabbed my wrist and sat me back down. "Look girl, I love you and I miss you. I'm sorry for cheating on you, but I promise I won't ever do you like that again. I love you too much and I don't wanna lose you," he stared into my eyes. I stared back at him, and then finally a smile spread across my face.

"I'm gonna give you one more chance, just one Konz. If you mess up again that's it. You need to be more responsible so that you won't break up our family," I told him, reciting Namiko's words that she gave me to say.

"Family? Ain't like we married baby girl," he chuckled.

"I know but umm I-I'm pregnant."

"Ah!" he hollered and jumped back away from me. He looked me up and down in horror.

"Konz, what is wrong with you?" I frowned.

"You're pre- pre- preg-" he stuttered.

"Preg-nant. Yes, I'm pregnant by you," I rolled my eyes and shook my head. He didn't say anything, and just stared at the carpet. "Konz?"

"Huh? Oh, umm, thank you?" he frowned.

"Thank you? What are you talking about?"

"Shit, I don't know what I'm supposed to say! This shit ain't ever happened to me before!" he shouted.

"You're supposed to be happy about it and tell me that you love me!" I yelled back to him.

"I don't know how I'm feeling Aniku. I don't know if I'm happy, angry, sad, or what. I just feel weird as hell," he replied.

"Weird why?" I quizzed and scooted closer to him.

"Cause I'm not meant to be anybody's father! I'm a brother, a homeboy, an uncle, not no fucking daddy! What kind of father would I be?" he spat.

"I'm not sure Konz, but it's too late for that. We're gonna have a baby, and you're gonna have to get it together," I cupped his face.

"Do you really even want a baby? I mean, it's still time to get rid of it right?" he smiled. I let go of his face and just stared at him.

"I thought you loved me." I squinted my eyes.

"I do Aniku, but a baby? Come on, neither one of us is even twenty-five yet." he tittered nervously.

"So you want me to get an abortion?"

"I just think that we have all the time in the world to make babies, and now just isn't a good time. I mean we're both pretty young, a-and we need to figure ourselves out before we have kids Aniku," he responded.

I covered my eyes with my hand, and sighed dejectedly. I couldn't believe I thought he would be welcoming when I told him. I wished I had never even gotten involved with him. I knew what type of guy he was from the get go.

"Aniku, talk to me," he broke the silence in the room.

"I'm gonna go Konz, make this the last time you contact me," I replied and stood up.

"So now you done because I don't wanna be a father right now?" he mugged me and threw his hands out at his side.

"It doesn't matter what you want! We're the ones who did this so we need to be mature about it! I'm not done because you don't want a baby right now. I'm done because you won't accept responsibility for it," I started to cry.

"Aniku-"

"Leave me alone," I said through gritted teeth before I left out.

I got into my car, and turned my phone off once I saw that Konz was blowing me up. I didn't know where to go right now. I didn't want to be home, and I didn't feel like dealing with neither Orianna nor Namiko. They would both think that they were right about Konz, and I didn't feel like dealing with that.

I sped to my parent's old home, and when I got there, I saw Kiyuki's car in the driveway. I quickly got out, because initially I came here to be alone but I missed her. I stuck my key in the door, and when I walked in, she was napping on the couch. Seeing her big belly reminded me of the little tiff I'd just had with Konz.

"Yuki," I whispered and shook her body lightly.

"Hunh?" she jumped and then smiled when she realized it was me, "Aniku, what are you doing here?" she questioned with squinted eyes.

"I just wanted to talk I guess. I actually came here to be alone, but I was kind of happy when I saw your car parked outside," I smiled and sat down on the couch.

"I'm surprised you're talking to me," she chuckled lightly.

"Why wouldn't I be?" I frowned.

"Oh you must have no idea," she shook her head. "I'm only gonna tell you because one, I'm tired of lying, and two, you're bound to find out sooner than later," she sighed. "All the stuff that happened to Namiko almost a year ago was my doing. And when Max and Deshawn got shot at that night, that was all me too," she looked at me. "Oh, the robberies of Max's product, all me," she nodded.

"Kiyuki, what is wrong with you? You need help. Why would you-"

"Save the speech Aniku," she put her hand up. "I've heard a speech from everyone and their damn mama. I've had my fix on speeches. If anybody has been hurt by my actions it's me," she exhaled.

"You? How are you suffering?" I frowned.

"Have you even wondered why I'm here and not with Deshawn? Well he doesn't want to be with me anymore because of what I've done. I was depressed about it, but just when I was starting to adjust, he comes over here and fucks me like he loves me, just to tell me it was a mistake in the morning," tears ran down her cheeks. "Then now, I'm living check to check, barely having enough money to buy groceries, and it's only gonna get worse when she gets here. Then to top it all off, everyone I love hates me," she cried.

"Kiyuki, I don't hate you. I don't like you sometimes, but I love you. Namiko loves you too but you can't blame her for being angry. You tried to kill her baby and her husband," I explained.

"I don't blame them for being mad, I just wish that they weren't," she sniffled.

"Yeah, I remember when the three of us used to be so close," I said in a low tone. "There was a time when nothing could break us up."

"The good ole days. It's nobody's fault but mine though," she shrugged.

"Then you need to be the one to fix it," I rubbed her back and she nodded.

DESHAWN

My little night I had with Kiyuki was a mistake like fuck. I knew I shouldn't have taken my ass over there, but I convinced myself that I was just going to check on the baby. In reality, I knew I visited her because I missed her and wanted to be in her presence.

As soon as I busted my nut, I felt like a fucking trader. Here I was fucking the same bitch that tried to kill me. When I thought about it, it made me wish that she wasn't pregnant by me. That's only when I was angry though. When I calmed down and came to my senses, I was happy that the baby was mine. It felt good to know that some parts of our relationship weren't a damn lie.

"Deshawn, earth calling," Evelyn smiled and snapped her fingers. We were out to dinner, and my stupid ass was too busy thinking about hoe ass Kiyuki.

"I'm sorry babe. I'm just a little tired," I smirked.

"I know you and Max have been working hard. But I'm sure the money makes it all worth it," she chuckled.

"You're right. You look beautiful tonight," I said. It felt like the first true thing I'd told her in a while.

"Thank you, you don't look too bad yourself," she replied. "You must be thinking about that DNA test still. I'm so sorry it turned out that way Deshawn," Evelyn shook her head.

"Well we all know how she is. I kind of knew it wasn't my baby," I shrugged and put some steak into my mouth. Yep, I sure did. I lied and told Evelyn that the baby came out not to be mine.

"True, but I'm just glad you came to your senses."

"If it wasn't for Cori I might've married her ass, so you're right," I laughed and she just cleared her throat uncomfortably. "You a'ight?" I asked. What did I say? I thought we were having a good conversation.

"You would've married her for real?" she questioned.

"What you want me to say Ev? Hunh? You want me to say that I never cared about her like that, and that I was only using her for sex? Hunh?" I frowned.

"I want you to be honest Deshawn! Y'all niggas ain't scared to carry guns and shoot people, but you're scared to tell a woman the truth," she scoffed.

"Alright," I wiped my mouth and threw my cloth napkin down. "You want the truth?" I inquired and she nodded. "I was in love with the girl when I was with her, that in fact *is* my baby, and yes I bought a ring with the intention of proposing to her, before I found out all this shit. Happy?"

"Excuse me? It *is* your baby?" she raised a brow. "So what was all that shit about her being a lying ass bitch, and the DNA test saying otherwise?" she grimaced.

"It was a lie. It was a fucking lie," I sipped my water and shrugged.

"You ain't shit Deshawn," she laughed and shook her head disap-pointingly.

"Then why are you with me?" I quizzed.

"Because I love you that's why. I just wish you could love me the same, but it's obvious you wanna be with Kiyuki nigga," she spat.

"Look Ev, who am I out to dinner with?"

"Me," she pouted.

"Then chill the fuck out then girl. Damn. This is why we broke up before. You overreact too fucking much!" I shouted in a low tone.

"Sorry."

"It's cool. Just relax though baby, I'm with you and nobody else," I took her hands into mine and caressed them.

"I know," she giggled.

After our little talk, dinner started to go better. We left and then headed home, because I was ready to fuck and go to sleep. Being awake seemed to be so fucking stressful, because all I thought about was Kiyuki Allen. I wished that we could be a family, but she fucked all that up.

I turned on the shower, and Evelyn walked in behind me butt naked. Her vanilla complexion was flawless, and her body was to die for as usual. She was thick in all the right places, and fit as fuck. For the first time in a while, I was thinking about her while being in her presence.

"Damn," I whispered and she smiled.

I flicked the other light switch, so that the red light could come on, and then I started to tongue her down. I backed her towards the shower, and then pushed the glass door back so that she could get in. When she turned around to step in, I smacked and grabbed her fat ass. I climbed in after her, and we continued to kiss passionately. I turned her around, and then gently bent her over. I was hard as a brick looking at the water run down her ass. I rubbed the tip of my dick against her opening, before finally plunging inside her.

"Ahh," we both moaned in unison.

I pumped her nice and fast, and the sound of our skin smacking was loud as fuck. I squeezed her ass roughly, and threw my head back in ecstasy.

"Deshawn baby," she whimpered and pressed one of her hands on the shower wall. I didn't say anything as I continued to ram into her sopping wet center.

"Ugghhh," I growled as I busted all inside her. "Shit," I panted as I slid out of her.

She stood up, turned around, and kissed my lips gently. She pulled back to look into my eyes, and then kissed me again. "I love you," she half smiled as she stared up into my eyes.

After we showered, we retired to bed and I couldn't sleep. I was really trying to make this shit work with Evelyn, but it became harder every day. The only time I didn't think about Kiyuki was when we were fucking.

I was just lying here in the bed staring at the ceiling, as Evelyn slept soundly next to me. I looked over at my phone on the nightstand, and grabbed it to text Kiyuki.

Me: *Are you awake?*

Kiyuki: *Nope, goodnight.*

I threw my phone back into the dresser, and just laid back down until I could fall sleep.

MAXIMILIAN

I was having a meeting with a guy I was gonna start supplying for the city of Troy. I heard good things about him, and I knew he and his team could make me a lot of money.

"So the way it works is we have a meeting stop where one of my people will deliver you the product. Be aware that they will be armed, and I need confirmation of receipt of product or money from both parties," I explained

"That's perfect, and you know I have no plans of trying to do you dirty. I know how you rock," he grinned.

"You never know man. People have been stupid enough to cross me in the past," I smirked and he shook his head. "So we will start small, and adjust until we see fit," I added and he nodded.

"Sounds like a plan boss," he cheesed.

"Hey baby," Esmeralda walked up and folded her arms.

She was wearing short ass shorts and a red halter-top. Her long curly weave was hanging down her back, looking like she just stepped out of the shower. Her jean shorts had her fat pussy on display, and her halter-top accentuated her breasts.

"Damn, this you?" Branden, my new business associate asked, as he eye fucked Esmeralda.

"Nah it's not. What's up Esme?" I looked up at her.

"Nothing, I just miss you baby. You haven't been answering my calls," she glared at me and then turned it into a smile.

"Well let me holla at you later, I need to finish this meeting," I fake smiled.

"Mmmm, a'ight," she smacked her lips and then switched off. I watched her ass as she walked away, and then broke my gaze.

"Damn, if that ain't you it should be." Branden commented as he watched her walk outside.

"Umm, I ain't really focused on women right now," I lied. I didn't like telling people I had a wife, because if some shit popped off, she would be the first person they went for.

"She seems hard not to think about," he chuckled.

"Help yourself," I gestured towards her.

We talked for a little bit more just to tie up some details, and then we parted ways. As I was walking out of the Bucharest Grill, Esmeralda was leaning up against the glass window of the restaurant.

"You still here?" I frowned.

"Yeah you said to wait," she giggled and stood up off the glass.

"I didn't say to wait. I said I would holla at yo ass later," I frowned. I didn't like this creepy shit she was on.

"Same shit," she waved me off. "So what's up with you, daddy? You haven't been hitting me back. I mean you called me to your little apartment a couple times, and then that was it," she cocked her head.

"A'ight, umm, sorry if you got the wrong impression but you know I ain't tryna be with you like that Esme. I have never tried to be in a relationship with you," I shrugged.

"So you used me is what you're saying?" she raised a brow.

"I wouldn't go that far, I mean, you enjoyed yourself too right?" I cheesed.

"Yeah because I thought we were gonna build something Max! You always do this shit to me!" she stomped and whined. "What am I not doing to where you don't wanna be with me?" she pouted.

"I don't know, shit, I just don't wanna be with you. I can't exactly pinpoint what it is, I just don't feel it," I replied. "I have to go though, Esme," I sighed.

"Go where? Let me come," she smiled.

"What? No, I'm going home to my wife," I nudged her back as she tried to push up on me.

"Where was she when I was riding your dick downtown?" she cheesed and ran her tongue over her teeth.

"And on that note, goodbye," I said and rushed to get into my car. I looked through my passenger window, and she was giving me an evil stare with her arms folded. I knew I shouldn't have fucked that girl.

AS SOON AS I WALKED INTO THE HOUSE, I SAW THE LIGHTS WERE very dim. I checked my back for my piece, and made sure it was secured. I walked slowly towards the stairs, and then suddenly Namiko appeared at the top. She was wearing lingerie that was white and lace. It was like a one-piece bathing suit, but open in the middle from her neck to her belly button, showing her beautiful skin. The crotch was completely see through, and I could see her bare kitten. I was at a loss for words at how sexy and beautiful she looked. She flung her long dark hair behind her shoulder, and then shifted her weight from one foot to the other. I saw she had white stilettoes on her feet, and shiny red nail polish.

"Namiko..." was all I could finally whisper.

She smirked and waved her pointing finger to tell me to come here. I started to jog up the stairs, and she turned around showing me that the little suit was a thong. I watch her perfectly round ass bounce, as she held onto my hand, leading me to the bedroom.

When we walked in, there were candles everywhere making the room smell like cotton candy or some shit. There was a bucket of ice with champagne in it, and strawberries and whipped cream next to it. I was still speechless. She led me to the bed, pushed me onto it, and then poured me a glass of the champagne and handed it to me. She leaned in close to my face as if she were gonna kiss me, but stopped right before our lips met. I watched her walk over to the stereo and turn on "Pussy" by Chris Brown.

Baby this is my pussy, I'ma fuck when I want to. Fuck when I want to, fuck when I want to. It's looking like that girl you know that I want to. Chris Brown sang, and the words were so true to me right now.

The room had a dark blue tint, as she swayed her sexy ass body to the music. She made eye contact with me, as she rocked her hips from side to side while running her hand down the front of her beautiful body. She threw her head back making her long hair fly. I wasn't even drinking the champagne, as I watched her closely. She turned to the side, dropped down, and wound her body as she came up. I started to wonder if she was ever a stripper in the past. She got on all fours, and then crawled to me slowly. Once she got to me, she ran her hands up my legs, and then swayed her body slowly as she came up. She strad-dled me, and then grabbed a strawberry to bite it. Her perfect teeth were so pretty. She grabbed another one, and then fed it to me. We didn't lose eye contact as I bit it. She took it then bit it after me. She then took the champagne out of my hand, and set it on the nightstand. She turned around and started to move her ass in my lap. I touched her smooth exposed back, and bit my lip as I watched her work her ass. Her body moved so perfectly with the Chris Brown's vocal style. I couldn't take it anymore. I felt like a fifteen-year-old boy who was about to bust before he even got his dick out. I grabbed her from behind, and then laid her on the bed. She giggled seductively, before I slipped my tongue into her mouth.

"You are so sexy Nami," I said in a low tone, as I tried to figure out how to get the lingerie off her.

"It's a zipper," she chuckled.

I flipped her over, and quickly unzipped her little contraption. I kissed down her sexy back, while roughly grabbing her ass. Once I made it to her ass, I licked inside and made my way down to her pussy. I positioned her to be face down, ass up, and then stood up to remove my clothes. All the while undressing, I stared at her pretty, pink pussy. Once I was I completely naked, I dropped down and took her clit into my mouth.

"Maaxx," she called out as I made love to her clit with my mouth.

I flicked my tongue over it, and then let my lips collapse over it before I sucked it. She tasted so good. I placed my palms on the back of her thighs, as I devoured her like a piece of fresh Popeye's chicken.

"Ahhh ugggh," she grunted softly as her juices spilled into my mouth.

I kept attacking her as if she didn't climax, as I enjoyed the sound of her screams and whimpers. I smacked her ass, and then squeezed it roughly to expose more of her pussy. I stuck the tip of my tongue into her, and then trailed it back down to her clit before sucking on it.

"Uhh uhh Maaxx, daddy please!" she begged me to stop just before cumming again.

I licked her clean, and watched with a smile as she tried to catch her breath. I rubbed the head of my dick on her clit, and she looked at me while biting her lip. I bent down and kissed the lips of her pussy very gently, making her moan loudly. I French kissed it a little more, as she whimpered like a little wounded animal. I stood back up, positioned the head of my dick at her opening and pushed it in inch by inch, as she balled the sheets up in her fists.

"You feel that shit," I said.

"Mm hmm," she cooed.

I plunged in and out of her nice and slow, while moving in a circular motion. I let my hands run amuck all over her small frame, as I pumped her. I smiled looking down at her biting her lip, and scrunching up her beautiful face.

"Ahh daddy I'm cumming," she purred and gushed on my rod.

I pushed her to the middle of the bed while still inside of her, and then pulled her to my chest. I sucked on her shoulders, while groping her breasts in my hands. I played with her nipples as I kissed the nape of her neck gently. Her pussy throbbed around my dick, while her juices ran down it. I slid out of her, and then laid on my back for her to mount my dick. She climbed atop me and slid down on my dick.

"Mmmm," we both mumbled in unison. She rocked her hips back and forth, while gliding up and down my dick nice and slow.

The love I had for this woman was unexplainable. She was beautiful, perfect, and everything I could ever want in a woman. I was blessed beyond belief to have her as my wife.

She put her small hand on my abs for leverage, and bounced a little faster. I pulled her upper body a little closer to me, so that I could suck her nipples. She bounced on my dick with her back arched, as I switched back and forth between her nipples. I sucked them hungrily, while cupping them in my hands.

"Ahh ahh!" she screamed out.

I cupped her ass roughly, and then humped upward fast, making us both explode. We stared at one another as we panted heavily. She finally dropped onto me, and we kissed passionately and nastily. I rubbed up and down her sweaty body, as we got lost in our kiss.

NAMIKO

I'd just finished registering for my senior year classes, and I was excited as hell. I had one more year before I was a college graduate. I would still have to get my master's in order to be in forensics like I planned, but I was hoping to just blow through that shit.

As I was walking to my car, I felt like someone was following me. I looked over my shoulder and saw a Hispanic chick walking behind me. She was on her phone, occupied, so I shrugged it off. Once I made it to the parking lot, I felt someone tap my shoulder.

"Hi, I'm Esmeralda," she stuck her hand out to shake mine.

"Namiko," I replied and shook her hand with a confused expression. I hadn't seen her in any of my classes, so I wasn't too sure why she was introducing herself to me.

"I'm just gonna come straight out with it. I'm pregnant by your husband," she smiled and then quickly wiped it off her face.

"Who is my husband?" I raised a brow and adjusted my backpack strap.

"Maximilian," she nodded.

"So what did you expect from this little parking lot revelation Esmeralda?" I asked.

"What did I expect?" she cocked her head.

"Yes, what did you expect from telling me this? Did you think that I was gonna believe my husband got a little rat like you pregnant, and then rush home to demand a divorce?" I chuckled lightly. I didn't care what this hoe said about Max, unless he told me out of his own mouth, I wasn't believing shit.

"Aye, watch ya mouth a'ight? I ain't no fucking rat! I was just trying to give you a heads up so that you won't be looking dumb out here while ya man has another family on the side," she pointed in my face.

"Watch where you point that finger a'ight?" I mocked her, "And you definitely are a rat if you would willingly lay on your back for a married man," I stared her in the eyes.

"He told me it was over," she exhaled and tried to force out some tears.

"And you believed him? Honey you don't need to be helping me not look stupid, you need to help yourself."

"Yes I believed him! Max has never lied to me before!" she shouted over the parking lot.

"Stop talking about my man like he's yours or something! I'm done with this conversation! Don't ever approach me again with your hoe revelations! If you do I'm gonna beat your ass!" I screamed and then headed towards my car.

I quickly cranked my shit up, and then sped to Starbucks. After getting my drink, I went home so that I could start dinner and spend some time with my baby. I hoped Max wouldn't be working all night, because he needed to hear about this shit! Any hoes he smashed in the past should not feel bold enough to approach his fucking wife!

"Hey cutie, you wanna come in the kitchen and help mommy cook?" I picked Baby Max up and kissed his fat face.

"I just changed his diaper," Dorothea smiled at me when she saw me check his pamper.

"Oh good, thank you," I replied and then went downstairs to the kitchen.

After washing my hands, I started to prepare the dinner. As I made my way around the kitchen, Chris Brown's velvety vocals spilled through my mini speaker.

"I must be getting wined and dined tonight," Maximilian walked into the kitchen smiling. He had on dark jeans, a black shirt, and black Nikes. His fade and facial hair were freshly trimmed, and he smelled so good.

"Why do you say that?" I giggled as he leaned down to kiss me.

"Cause you got CB on and shit. Maybe I got the wrong impression. I'm spoiled after that little striptease you gave me," he bit his lip and pinched my ass.

"I knew I shouldn't have done that," I joked and lightly tapped his rock hard abs.

"Nah, you definitely *should* have, and *should* do it again. I may have some cash for you," he winked with his sexy ass. I just blushed and turned my attention back to the food I was making.

"Well you better make sure you have the right bills, because I will take nothing less than fifty dollar bills," I cracked and he chuckled.

"A saddity ass dancer," he commented. "Hey man," he scooped Baby Max up and kissed his face.

"Max, who the hell is Esmeralda?" I quizzed as I laid the fish in the pan.

"Uh, umm, why?" he questioned.

"Because I wanna know. Who is she?" I repeated.

He exhaled heavily and then said, "She was this girl that I used to mess around with. It was never nothing serious, just fucking," he shrugged and put our son back into the swing.

"Well she approached me today, saying she's pregnant by you," I looked at him.

"Where was this? And what time did this happen?" he asked and then followed it with an angry chuckle.

"Today, at school. We got into a little screaming match," I replied and continued cooking the food. He didn't say anything, so I turned off the music to give him some peace.

"Sorry about that. It won't happen again," he sighed and then folded his arms across his strong chest.

"That's all you have to say?" I frowned.

"Namiko, I'm gonna take care of it. That's all you need to know," he glared back at me. I shook my head and walked past him to get something out of the cabinet. He grabbed me by my waist, and pulled me close. "Quit being so fucking mean, before I have to discipline yo ass," he grinned and made my clit throb.

"Move," I whined and giggled as he kissed on my neck.

"I love you," he smirked.

"I love you too," I whispered and touched his smooth dark caramel skin.

I hoped that today was the last time I had an encounter with Esmeralda. If Maximilian didn't take care of her, we were gonna have a big problem. I was so over having to fight people off to be with him. Yes, I loved him, but we both needed to stop letting people slide.

KIYUKI

„Here she is Ms. Allen," the nurse smiled as she walked my daughter over to me, after cleaning her up. She was so pretty, but I couldn't really tell if she looked like Deshawn or me yet. We decided to name her, Mai Deshawn Sinead.

"You wanna hold her?" I asked Deshawn and he just stared at her for a couple seconds before responding.

"Ye-yeah sure," he half smiled and walked closer. He picked her up carefully, and then stared at her with his mouth open. "She's beautiful," he said in a low tone.

"Of course she is," I chuckled and then laid my head back on the pillow. I was so tired, and in so much pain.

"So how are we gonna do this whole co-parenting thing?" he asked as he laid Mai in her plastic crib.

"I really don't want to talk about that right now. However, I do need you to help for the first couple of weeks, because I won't be too mobile," I sighed.

"You and Mai can come stay with me during that time," he offered.

"No, we need to be settled in the place that she and I are gonna be living at permanently," I replied.

"So what are we gonna do after the first couple of weeks?" he quizzed.

"Well honestly, I think you should just come over the house when you want to see her. Once she gets to be about six months, then you can take her."

"What? Fuck that! After those first couple of weeks I should be able to take her to my home," he spat.

"I said no Deshawn," I frowned.

"You're only doing this because you're jealous of Evelyn," he scoffed and shook his head at me.

"I'm not jealous of anybody Deshawn. I don't think she should be without me until she's at least six months. That's all there is to it," I shrugged.

"Well, if you think this is gonna make me be with yo' ass you are sadly mistaken," he stared me in the eyes to show me he meant business.

"That's the least of my worries, but thank you for clarifying," I sighed and then closed my eyes. I was too tired to argue with him.

"I'm glad you know. I don't want anything to do with you outside of this baby, aight?" he raised his brows.

"Yep," I nodded without opening my eyes.

"Our relationship was never really anything anyway. I don't know what I was thinking by trying to make something happen with a girl like you. The only thing I don't regret about us is my daughter. I just wish she had a different mother," he barked.

"Deshawn, if this is an attempt to hurt my feelings and make me feel bad, congratulations you've accomplished that. Now please stop," I said as tears slid down my cheeks.

I was really trying to keep myself from being depressed, but he was making it hard. Especially, when he showed up at my house that evening just to sleep with me and say it was a mistake. I was in physical and mental pain right now.

"I'm just being honest," he said in a low tone, as he looked down at his hands.

"Heeyyy," Aniku smiled as she entered the room with flowers. I quickly wiped my eyes, and sat up as much as I could.

"Thank you," I chuckled as she handed me the flowers in her hand. I pushed my long dark hair behind my ears, and then sniffed them.

"Sorry I couldn't get Nami to come," she said and caressed my head.

"It's cool, thanks for trying though," I exhaled. I tried making up with Namiko, but she said she didn't want to hear from me until I dropped my baby so she could beat my ass.

"You're welcome. Oh sorry, hi Deshawn," she half smiled at him, and then sat down in the empty chair.

"What's up," he said and then looked away. "I'm gonna go check on my girl, and then get some food. Anybody want anything?" he quizzed and then stood up.

"No," I replied and Aniku shook her head no.

"His girl? Did he really have to say that part?" Aniku rolled her eyes once he left.

"Yeah, I guess he is just trying to make me understand that he and I will never be," I said.

"Why? Have you been pushing up on him?" she turned her lip up.

"Hell no! I told him that he couldn't take the baby over to his house without me until she was six months, and I guess he thinks I'm saying that because I'm jealous of Evelyn," I exhaled heavily.

"Are you?"

"I'm jealous because I love him, but that is not why he can't take Mai over to his home. I just think before six months she shouldn't be away from me," I shrugged.

"Is he still saying mean things to you?" she asked.

"You know he is. I can't count how many times he has said he regrets being with me, and will never do it again."

"I think he's saying it more so to convince himself than you," she raised a brow.

"Yeah right!" I chuckled.

"Just wait on it," she nodded.

I talked with Aniku for a little bit longer, and then she left to get me some Japanese food. After bringing it up to me, she headed home. In the middle of eating, Deshawn came back into the room. He was wearing a gray jogger suit, and had a duffle bag on his shoulder.

"I thought you said you weren't hungry," he frowned.

"I wasn't but after a while I got hungry," I shrugged and kept my eyes on my food.

"You could've called me to bring you something Kiyuki."

"I'm sorry Deshawn," I sighed and still didn't look up from my food. What the fuck was his problem? He should be happy that I didn't bother him during his time with Evelyn.

He didn't respond to me, he just started to lay out the pullout bed. What the fuck was he doing? He went into the cabinet, and then pulled a blanket and pillow out of it. I was gonna speak up, but the nurse came in.

"Ms. Allen, hello Mr. Sinead," she smiled and Deshawn nodded. "I just wanted to ask if you've breast fed since earlier?" she quizzed.

"Yes, while my sister was here I did," I replied and watched her write on her chart.

"Okay, and did you still want the hospital dinner? I see you have some food."

"Yes please, Japanese food doesn't stick to the stomach." I half joked and she chuckled. Deshawn was sitting on the pullout bed watching us intently.

"Okay, that will be here in about an hour," she said and then looked at my daughter as she slept soundly. "Beautiful baby," she grinned. "Hit the button if you need anything," she added before skipping out.

"Deshawn, you're spending the night?" I quizzed.

"Yeah, is that a problem?" he raised his brow.

"Well, I just don't want your girlfriend coming up here with no bullshit. I'm not exactly in the condition to fight," I said as I put my finished food in the plastic bag.

"Well she is *my* girlfriend, so you let me handle and worry about that," he said and then adjusted the pillow on the bed. I just nodded and laid my head back on the pillow.

KONZ

TWO WEEKS LATER...

I was missing Aniku like crazy. We hadn't talked to one another since she told me about the baby. I didn't understand why she didn't get where I was coming from. It's not like I was saying anything bad about her, I was just trying to get her to see that I didn't want a baby at this moment. I was trying to be honest with her.

I loved Aniku, but I wanted to develop our relationship more before bringing a baby in this world. I felt like the baby would split us up for good, and I didn't want that at all. On top of that, I wasn't ready to be anybody's daddy. I had no idea how I wanted to make money, and I needed to figure that out before I had a family of my own. Yeah I worked for Maximilian right now, but I didn't know if that was something I was gonna keep doing or not. I'll be damned if I'm gonna be out here with a girl and child with no fucking money, or begging my brother to pay my rent and bills. That shit seemed cool at first, but now I wanted to be doing my own thing.

Today I was gonna drop by my brother's house in hopes of talking to her. I'd tried calling her over, and even catching her in her school parking lot, but none of that shit worked.

I pulled up to Max's crib, and checked my appearance before

getting out of the car. *When you leave here, y'all need to be back together,* I told myself as I walked up the roundabout driveway.

"Oh, hello Mr. Davis," Max's nanny Dorothea answered the door.

"Hey, what's up? Is Aniku here?" I questioned as I walked in and stood in the foyer.

I looked around it a little bit, and admired the sparkling marble floors. It was obvious that she had just cleaned it.

"Yes, she is upstairs in her room. I can go get her for you," she offered.

"Nah, you good. I will just visit her. Is my brother or Namiko here?" I quizzed before I started up the stairs.

"No, they took Baby Max to the movies," she smiled and then picked up a basket of laundry. I nodded and jogged to the top of the stairs.

I walked down the hall until I reached Aniku's room. I heard Rihanna playing from her room, and then took a deep breath. I twisted the knob, and saw she was on her bed looking at a magazine. When I closed the door behind me, she looked up. She paused the music on her phone, and we just stared in silence.

"How are you?" I finally asked, and then sat on the edge of her bed.

"I'm fine," she replied in a low tone. She closed the magazine, and then sat up all the way.

"I missed you," I half smiled. She just stared at me emotionless. The pillow was covering her chest as she hugged it tightly. "Aniku baby, I didn't mean to hurt ya feelings or whatever," I said.

"Too late," she replied.

"I'm sorry aight? I just wanted you to see that neither of us are ready to have a baby-"

"If you came here to try and convince me to get an abortion, you can leave Konz. I'm not getting one. Stop asking me and stop trying to talk to me about it," she spat.

"Aniku, we ain't ready for this. You don't even have a fucking job!" I shouted.

"You sure didn't care about me not having a job when you were fucking me with no hat!" she yelled. I massaged my closed eyes, and then sighed.

"I know that we are both responsible for what happened here, but don't you think we need a little more time together? A little more time in general?" I frowned.

"Time for what? To grow up?"

"Yes, to grow up and to get our shit together. Wouldn't you much rather have your degree, a good job, and even a husband when you have a baby?" I rubbed her leg.

"Of course Konz, but sometimes things don't work out the way we plan them. My parents did it the right way and it still ended up going downhill," she shook her head.

"What you talking about? You told me your parents were middle class," I furrowed my brows.

"Yeah, they were when they had *two* incomes. After my mother died from breast cancer, my dad was forced to pay all the bills using his one paycheck. That's what drove him to drink and hit us," she responded.

"Us? I thought he only hit Namiko?" I questioned further.

"Well he hit her the most, but on rare occasions he would bring it Kiyuki's and my way. But regardless, before all that stuff, my father would never put his hands on us. So see, they planned everything and at first, it was going accordingly, but then it all changed. You have to be prepared for things to not go the way you imagined them Konz," she said. "So yes, I would much rather be a dentist when I have a baby, but that's not what God planned for me. I have to take responsibility for what I've done, and for the path that I chose to go down," she added.

"When did you get so wise?" I quizzed and squeezed her thigh.

"Uh, more like Namiko is the wise one," she giggled. Her beautiful chocolate skin was glowing, and I leaned over and kissed her cheek.

"Yeah, my brother got a good one on his hands," I paused. "So I guess I'm gonna be a daddy," I exhaled and stared at her pink carpet.

"I guess you are. It's gonna be okay Konz. Worse things have happened to you," she responded.

"Ain't that the fucking truth," I scoffed. "But one of the good things that happened to me was you Ms. Allen," I grinned.

"I know that! But if you don't get it together, I won't be with you anymore," she said.

"I'm gon' get it together. Ya boy is gon' get it together," I sighed. "Unlike your father, I can adjust aight?" I rubbed her cheek.

"Hey, he may have been a basket case on the tail end of his life, but that's still my daddy! Watch your mouth," she joked.

"Come here," I said and moved the pillow out of her arms. I pulled her close, and then dipped my tongue into her mouth. We continued to kiss until I was on top of her and between her legs.

EVELYN

Here it was another night where I was sleeping alone. I'd text Deshawn at 8pm, and it was now 11pm with no response. I couldn't help but feel dumb about our relationship. I felt like I was trying to make something happen that just wasn't meant to happen. I knew very well where Deshawn was. He was over Kiyuki's house playing the Huxtables. Ever since their daughter Mai was born, it seemed like there was no room for me. All he did was attend meetings and shit all day with Maximilian, and then spend the rest of the night with Kiyuki and his daughter. He would make time for me here and there, but it was only when I made a big deal about him spending too much time with that slut and his baby.

"Fuck this," I said and threw the covers off me.

I'd just finished watching a movie where this girl was preaching about going to get your man, and that's what I was going to do. Kiyuki was not about to take him from me again.

I threw on some tennis shoes, tights, and a spaghetti strapped top. I grabbed my jacket, and then my keys as well. First, I sped to Deshawn's crib, and just as I suspected, his car was nowhere to be found. I immediately busted a U-turn so that I could go to Namiko's old house, where Kiyuki was staying. If his car was there I was gonna go ape shit. His best bet was to be somewhere with Max.

Back and forth with my conscience, back and forth with that bullshit. Back and forth with your nonsense, I keep saying I'ma leave you. Back and forth with that drama, bitches adding more bullshit, and I'm just counting yo' condoms, one day I'ma learn. Christina Milian's "Liar" blasted through my car speakers as I sang along. This song was just speaking to me right now, and adding fuel to my already burning fire.

I pulled up to Kiyuki's home, and just like I thought, his car was right there and parked behind hers. I shut the engine off, took a big drink of water, and then hopped out. I didn't want any alcohol because I didn't want to relive the time I almost killed him. I re-did my bun, and made sure it was good and tight as I walked up the driveway.

BOOM!

BOOM!

BOOM!

I heard light movement, which made me bang on the door even harder. Then I heard the baby cry loudly, as I waited impatiently for the door to be answered. Someone peeked through the peephole in the door, and then finally it flung it open.

"What the hell Evelyn?" Deshawn stepped outside and closed the door behind him.

"Excuse me? What the fuck are you doing here? It's 11:45 at night nigga!" I shouted loud as fuck. The baby's cries had subsided by now.

"Lower your voice. I'm here because my baby is here," he spat.

"The baby is sleep and you should be at home or with me. Not here with that hoe ass bitch!" I screamed. I was so angry. I pushed his ass backward, and then was about to punch him but he grabbed my wrists.

"It's a wrap," he stated calmly.

"A wrap? Why because-"

"Can you guys take this home or anywhere that isn't my doorstep please?" Kiyuki opened the door. "I just got my daughter back to sleep, and I'd like to get some along with her," she folded her arms.

"You fucking bitch!" I shouted and charged towards her, but Deshawn grabbed me roughly. She stood in the doorway with her arms folded, and shook her head at me as Deshawn carried me to my car. "You cannot do this!" I yelled as I started to cry.

"Evelyn this ain't meant shorty. It's over, we're just not compatible," he said in a pleading tone. "You said that you could handle me having a baby with Kiyuki, but you can't," he panted.

"Yes I can, but you're doing it all wrong Deshawn! You're not supposed to stay out all day and then spend all night with her! You're supposed to come over here, spend time with the baby until she falls asleep, and then go home!" I cried. "Why are you still spending time here if the baby is asleep?" I stared up into his eyes.

"Evelyn-"

"Be honest Deshawn, please. Don't I deserve that much?" I sniffled and wiped my nose. "Do you wanna be with her? You love her? You can tell me Deshawn, I won't even judge you," I added.

He sighed and then stared off into the street for a little bit. "Yeah man, I love her," he dropped his head, and then looked back up to see my reaction.

"How?" I frowned in confusion. "After all that she's done to you, how could you want to be with her?"

"I don't want to want to be with her Ev, I just do. And the more I see her being a mother to my baby, the more I want her," he shook his head at himself.

"So are you gonna be with her?" I questioned.

"I can't do that," he exhaled. "She did the unthinkable. How would I look being with a girl who tried to have me killed?" he chuckled lightly, and then wiped the smile from his sexy face.

"I'm not a Kiyuki fan, but it was before she dated you Deshawn. So if you want to be with her, you should. You can't live your life based on what people think of you, or you'll never be happy," I told him shocking myself.

I wanted him, but not if he wanted someone else. I cared about him, and I could see how unhappy and angry he was because he couldn't be with her. It hurt me, but I would get over it in time.

"So you wouldn't think I was some pussy ass nigga if I took her back?" he half smiled at me and I shook my head no, while smiling.

"I know you Deshawn, and you're not even close to being a pussy ass nigga. You're dumb as hell sometimes, but not a pussy," I joked.

"You know I'm gone always have love for you right?" he ran his finger under my chin.

"Likewise," I responded and stared up into his eyes.

MAXIMILIAN

I was lying down, tossing a stress ball up in the air. I was just waiting patiently for shit to pop off so I could end all this bullshit. I caught the ball as it descended down, and then picked up my wrist to look at my watch. It was 4:55pm, and show time would be around 5pm. I continued to toss the ball in the air, as I waited calmly for the minutes to fly by.

"Ma!" I heard a voice yell once it was 5:02pm. I chuckled to myself as the voice repeated itself. The footsteps came closer to the bedroom I was in, but I didn't budge. "What the fuck are you doing in my room? And where is my mother?" Esmeralda spat.

"Close the door behind you, and watch your tone," I ordered and sat up in the bed. She stared at me for a couple moments, and then did as I asked.

"Explain yourself Max," she folded her arms across her breasts.

"No you explain your fucking self! Why the fuck are you approaching my wife telling her you're fucking pregnant! What the fuck is wrong with yo' ass!" I shouted.

"I knew it would get your attention," she chuckled and dropped her duffle bag onto her floor.

"You knew it would get my attention," I nodded as I repeated her words. "It got the wrong kind of attention baby girl. See I'm angry, very angry," I stared her in the eyes.

"I can fix that," she smirked and caressed my shoulder.

"Nah move!" I shoved her lightly. I stood up off the bed and towered over her. "You pissed me off with that bullshit you pulled on my wife. I know you got more tricks up your hoe ass sleeve too," I hissed.

"Maybe, but it's only because I'm tired of you using me papi. You know how I feel about you. I'll even settle for being a sister wife," she joked. At least I hoped she was joking.

"Oh you would hunh?" I smirked.

"Absolutely. Just until you realize on your own that I'm the woman you want to be with," she giggled seductively.

"Esme, you know I ain't never even looked at you as the wifey type. Even if I were to have a second wife, it wouldn't be you," I smiled.

"I'd like to think that you don't have a choice Max," she raised a brow and spidered her fingers up my bicep.

"How so?" I questioned.

"I guess you've forgotten that I have some information on you that you wouldn't like to get out. Remember, you killed my brother," she leaned up and whispered into my ear.

"I had a feeling you'd try and go that route," I grinned.

"I don't wanna have to blackmail you baby, but you're not really giving me a choice here," she responded.

"And to think I had a surprise for you," I chuckled.

"A surprise?" she bucked her eyes. "What kind of surprise?" she smiled and put her hand on her hip.

"Open the closet," I winked. She stared at me for a couple seconds, and then went to the closet to open it.

"Ahhhhh!!!!" she screamed so loud I thought the windows would break. "Ma!" she cried as she took in the sight of her mother hanging in the closet. When she turned to me, I had a gun right in her face.

"I told you that you didn't wanna make me angry bitch. I tried to let you off the hook when I offed Cobra, but you just had to overstep your boundaries, just like him," I shook my head.

"Max please," she cried with her hands up.

PHEW! PHEW!

I pumped two silent shots into her dome, and then pulled out my phone to call Dagger and his team. After telling me he'd be here in about ten minutes, I decided to do a little wiping of my own. I wiped down Esmeralda's whole room, and by the time I was done, Dagger and the crew had arrived. I sat outside in my car until they finished, and then drove home.

❧

I WALKED INTO MY BEDROOM, AND HEARD THE SHOWER RUNNING IN the bathroom. I stripped down to nothing, and then walked in to see Namiko showering. I opened the glass door, and she jumped but then smiled when she saw it was me.

"You scared me," she said as I stepped in behind her. I planted kisses on her neck and shoulders, making her throw her head back in ecstasy. "When did you get here?" she whispered.

"Literally like ten minutes ago," I replied before I turned her around to tongue her down.

"Mmmm," a moan escaped her mouth as we kissed passionately.

I picked her small body up, and then slid her down onto my dick slowly. She felt so good, and every time I entered her, a shiver would crawl down my spine. I sucked on her neck as I plunged in and out of her slowly.

"Maaaxx," she called out in pleasure.

I pulled her full bottom lip into my mouth, and then did the same with the top lip. I slipped my tongue into her mouth, and let our tongues dance together as I sped up my strokes. The warm water only heightened our senses, bringing my orgasm quicker.

"I love you so much Maximilian," she whimpered as her juices spilled out onto my dick.

Her pussy was now wetter, and I couldn't take much more. I rammed into her, as we both screamed out. I gripped her little plump ass in my hands and made her pussy lips spread some, before we both exploded. I brought my hands up around her torso, and hugged her tightly as we indulged in a long kiss. I let her down, and then we began to wash each other off.

After our long shower, we went to the bedroom to change into our pajamas. Namiko made us both some tea, and then we turned on Netflix.

"Have you seen your sister's baby?" I asked and she shook her head no. "You don't want to?" I quizzed.

"Oh I will, but not yet," she smirked and then winked at me.

NAMIKO

I fed Baby Max after bathing him, and put him into his playpen. I ate some cereal, and ran upstairs to get dressed. I slipped into my workout gear, and then crossed out today's event on my calendar.

"Hey Thea, I will be back in about an hour or two. MJ is in his room," I smiled at her.

"Okay Mrs. Davis," she nodded and went back to folding laundry.

I rushed out of the house, and hopped into my car. I sped through Detroit, remembering my goal. I'd been waiting for today to happen for a very long time. I felt like once this was over, I could finally move on and be happy with my life.

I pulled up to my destination, parked across the street, and then jogged across the street. I banged on the door, and then waited for it to open. My leg bounced impatiently after I banged on the door again.

"Namiko, why do-"

WHAM!

I punched the shit out of Kiyuki. She stumbled backwards, and I continued fucking her up. She grabbed my hair, and then let go to grab my wrists, but I was still going in on her. She finally caught my wrists, and pushed me off. I charged her again, and slapped the dog shit out of her bloody face.

"Alright! Namiko I'm sorry!!" she screamed and cried hysterically. I just stared at her as I panted heavily. "I'm sorry!" she sobbed as blood dripped from her lip and nose.

"Kiyuki we're supposed to be sisters!" I shouted. "No one is supposed to be able to come between us, especially a man!"

"I know Nami, and I don't know what else to say besides I'm sorry. I'm sorry for fucking up your car, for having coffee grounds thrown on you, and I'm sorry for getting you jumped while pregnant with Baby Max. But now I am begging you to forgive me Nami," she sniffled and touched her bloody nose with her forearm.

"Why should I forgive you?" I grimaced.

"Because, like you said, we're sisters. Don't be like me and disregard our relationship. Can't you see I'm suffering right now? I can't take this shit anymore!" she cried like a newborn. "I'm alone, I'm depressed, and I hate myself, but I can't sulk because I have to be a mother. I know I deserve this but please, I need someone to have some mercy on me!" she wailed as she slid down onto the floor. As hard as I tried to be angry, I couldn't. She looked so broken, and I'm sure that because she'd just had a baby it was even worse.

"Kiyuki, stop crying," I got on the floor, grabbed her, and hugged her tightly. "I love you. That's why I need you to understand that what you did was pointless. A man is not more important than the love we have for one another," I said as I held her head against my chest.

"I know Namiko. I don't want you to hate me. I want us to be like before," she sniffled.

"Well, that's the good thing about being sister's right? We fight and then we forgive," I smiled down into her face.

"Thank you," she replied and then wrapped her arms around my torso. She laid her head back on my chest. "So where is my niece?" I quizzed.

"She's sleeping, you wanna see her?" she beamed. She looked so happy to be talking about her.

"Yeah I do, but let's clean your face first," I half smiled and she nodded.

We got up and headed to her bathroom to clean her face up. Once we were finished, she led me to my old bedroom, which she had turned into a nursery.

"Wow Kiyuki, how much did all of this work cost?" I asked as I looked around the beautiful room.

"I don't really know. Deshawn paid for all of this," she shrugged. I followed her to the crib, and looked over at my beautiful niece sleeping.

"She's so pretty Yuki. She looks just like you and Deshawn," I whispered and chuckled softly. I wanted to hold her, but I didn't want to wake her.

"Thank you," she smiled as she looked down at her.

"So have you guys figured out how you're going to co-parent?" I questioned as we walked back to her room.

"Well, he is usually over here a lot, but once she turns six months, I will let him take her over to his house," she responded as she fidgeted.

"Did you know that he and Evelyn broke up?" I raised a brow and her head shot up. She searched my eyes for a couple moments before speaking.

"Really? I had no idea," she said.

"Yeah, Evelyn told me they broke up because he wants to be with you," I grinned and she just shook her head.

"It doesn't seem that way."

"Yeah, Aniku told me he talks down to you. But I agree with her that he only does that to convince himself," I rubbed her hand.

"Well until he can grow up, we won't find out," she fake smiled and we laughed. "I need to focus on myself and my baby, not chasing after some little boy," she added.

"I feel you," I laid back on her bed.

We talked for a little longer, until Mai woke up. When she did, I held her for a little while, until Kiyuki finished cooking lunch. We ate together, and then I waited until she put the baby to sleep.

"I will be back to see you tomorrow," I kissed her cheek before leaving.

"I'll be waiting," she cheesed.

"And don't forget, I love you," I said as I stood in her front doorway.

"I love you too Nami," she half smiled at me.

I drove home, and on the way there, I couldn't help but smile. I missed having all my sisters to lean on. I really hoped that all of this shit would bring us closer together. Maybe all the events that transpired were a way to bring us closer more genuinely than before. Whatever the case was, I just hoped and prayed that this was the end of all the drama within our little family. Don't get me wrong though, punching her ass a couple times did feel good.

KIYUKI

A WEEK AND A HALF LATER...

I was tired as hell today. I'd been running errands for the longest, and then I went with a realtor to look at some condos. Yeah Deshawn agreed to pay the mortgage on this house, but I was tired of depending on him. I hated to lose my parents' house, but it just wasn't in the budget.

Mai and I were coming home from the grocery store. Thank God I'd gotten a good job before I gave birth, because I was able to get money from pregnancy leave. I put my key into the door, and then kicked it open. As I carried my baby in, I took in the atmosphere. The room was lit with red candles, and there were red roses all over the living room. There was a table with three chairs, and dinnerware on it. I looked at Deshawn because I was confused what all of this was for. Last time I checked, he hated my guts. Or as he put it, the only reason I was alive was because of our baby.

"Close the door and come here," he smiled. He was dressed in an all-white tuxedo, and looking so fresh.

I walked over to him, while still holding my daughter, and then sat on the couch. It was quiet except for the little baby noises Mai was making.

"Kiyuki, first I want to apologize for the way that I've been treating you for the past six or seven months. Yeah you did some terrible shit to Maximilian, your sister, and me but you didn't deserve to hear some of the things I said to you. For a while, I've tried to hate you, and I've tried to make myself believe that I was over our relationship, and that it meant nothing. It seemed like the more I did that though, the stronger I felt for you. I had my mind made up that I was gonna force myself, no matter what, to move on and be with someone else. But no matter how many women I entertained, I always thought about you. I was always comparing them to you. I hope that my unkind words haven't made you feel bad about yourself, because despite some of your actions, you're a great woman baby. The fact that when we all found out what you did, you didn't try and scheme your way out of it, or most importantly hurt my sister, says a lot. I do know that you had something done to Kateria, but I'm glad you came to your senses before doing anything else," he sighed and looked away. Mai made a noise, so he looked down at her and smiled. "I love how refreshing, wild, and fun you are but I also love that you know how to tone it down and let a man be a man," he added. "So I'm saying all this to let you know that," he took a deep breath and then got off the couch onto his knee, causing me to gasp faintly. "I love you Kiyuki and I want you to be my wife," he finished and looked up into my eyes.

"Wife?" I whispered.

"Yes, my wife," he repeated and retrieved a ring from his pocket. It appeared to be about thirteen karats, but I didn't exactly know. "So is that a yes? Or a fuck you nigga, you're too late?" he half joked.

"Umm, I-"

"Don't make me beg, because I will damn sure beg you," he smirked.

"Well, you were pretty mean to me, and you did hurt my feelings making me cry myself to sleep for countless nights," I said and he displayed a worried expression. "But if you can forgive me, then it's only right that I forgive you. And if we can promise each other to never do what we did again, then I would be honored to be your wife," I grinned as his jaw hit the floor.

"So for real?" he beamed and I nodded. "And I promise you that I will never put you down again," he added and slid the ring onto my finger.

"And I promise to never betray you, and to always have your back," I half smiled.

He took the baby out of my arms, and laid her gently on her stomach since she had fallen asleep. He stood up, and then yanked me up off the couch. Before I could speak, he slipped his tongued into my mouth and kissed me hungrily.

"Damn I missed doing that," he said in a low tone. "Sit down so I can bring the food," he said and held the chair out for me to sit.

He returned a couple moments later, with a plate of his spicy barbecue ribs that he made with Dr. Pepper. They were complemented with mashed potatoes, and asparagus. He opened a bottle of champagne, and was about to pour me some, but I stopped him.

"I can't drink because I have to breast feed," I giggled.

"Well I bought cider, you want that?" he quizzed and I nodded.

After he poured my drink, we scarfed the food down. I'd missed his little rib dish, even though I thought it was dumb as hell when he first told me the recipe. Once we were done, I put Mai into her crib, and then turned up the baby monitor once Deshawn and I entered the bedroom.

Deshawn closed the door, and then neared me. The room was dark, but had just enough light so that we could see one another. We sucked each other's lips, as he lifted my shirt up and off. He unhooked my bra, and then dropped down to unbutton my jeans. He pulled them down, along with my panties, and then I sat on my bed so he could get them past my feet. He stood up and undressed, as I watched him closely. I hadn't had sex since that night he came over and played me, so I was dripping already. He pushed me back, and then we got into the middle of the bed.

"Mmmm," I cooed as he kissed my neck, collarbone, and then my breasts.

He kissed down my body, and then on my inner thighs. He took my clit into his mouth, and sucked it gently. Every so often, he would slip his tongue into my hole, before bringing his mouth back to my clit.

"Uhh, uhh," I moaned as I released into his mouth. He licked me clean, and then went right back to attacking. "Mmmm, uggh," I grunted softly as I came again.

He stood up on his knees, and I sat up to suck his dick but he stopped me. He laid me back down, and then lowered himself between my legs. He stared into my eyes, and then planted a soft kiss on my lips. He placed my legs in the nook of his arms, and then I felt the head of his dick at my opening. He pushed in and made me jump, but it went nowhere.

"Damn, they sewed you up good," he chuckled and then looked down between my legs. He licked his fingers, and then put them down between my legs. He slowly plunged them into me, and moved in and out. "There we go," he bit his lip while staring at me making sex faces. I came again on his fingers, and he slipped them out to lick them.

He placed my legs back in the nooks of his arms, and then pressed the head of his dick at my opening with more force.

"Uhh, ahh!' I whimpered as he entered me inch by inch.

"Oh fuck Yuki," he groaned as he made his way inside me. I felt like I was getting my virginity taken. "Shit babe," he whispered and sucked on my lips.

"Aahh, uhhh, ahhh," I purred as he thrust inside me. I was finally starting to feel pleasure after so much pain. "Don't go fast," I added once I felt him speed up a little.

He started tonguing me down again, as he continued to pump me slowly. I gushed on his rod, and he pinned my hands above my head. He started to go in a circular motion, hitting my spot repeatedly.

"Cum for me babe," he said in a low tone. "Ahhh," he moaned.

"Uggghh," I released again. I was so drenched down there that I was sure we would have to change the sheets before going to bed.

"Arrgghh," Deshawn called out as he shot his seeds inside me. "I love you," he panted and dropped down onto me. He slipped his tongue in my mouth, and we just laid there kissing passionately.

ANIKU

Tonight my sisters and I were gonna have dinner together. I can't remember the last time we all did something together. Before Kiyuki and Namiko became estranged, we never had the funds to go anywhere or do anything. I was excited because I missed the good times we would have together.

"You ready?" Namiko peeked her head into the room. She was wearing a strapless yellow dress, and her hair and nails were freshly done.

"Just about," I replied as I smoothed down my white skirt. I wore a flowy orange top to match because I felt like people could tell I was pregnant if I didn't.

"Aniku, you're only two months pregnant. Nothing is showing," Namiko giggled and folded her arms across her breast. Just then, Maximilian came up behind her and hugged her tightly.

"Where are you guys going to eat?" he inquired.

"To Joe Muer's," Namiko and I responded in unison. Max nodded his head, and then craned his neck around to kiss Namiko.

"See you later," Namiko said and then waved me to come on.

We climbed into her Porsche, and then sped out of the driveway to pick up Kiyuki. She turned on a Young Thug mixtape, and we began to dance and sing along.

"Aren't you excited?" I smiled over at her.

"Excited for what?" she frowned in confusion.

"Excited to have dinner like the old times," I giggled and saw a smirk appear on her face.

"I can't lie; it does feel good to not have so much beef going on between Kiyuki and I. I just hope that she has really changed, and that she doesn't get pissed off and do crazy shit," she sighed.

"Don't be negative Nami. Plus, I think she has really turned over a new leaf. Especially now that she has Mai," I nodded because I was sure that I was right. "Can't you tell the difference in her demeanor?" I asked.

"Yeah you're right, I can see. Before you could feel the bad energy radiating off of her," Namiko nodded to herself as she turned onto Kiyuki and Deshawn's street.

"How is Evelyn doing?" I quizzed. I wanted to find out before Kiyuki got into the car.

"She is actually doing okay. She's much better than the last time that this happened. I think it's because she is talking to this guy from our last year's Biology class."

"Well they always say; the best way to get over one nigga is by getting friendly with another!" I half joked and we laughed.

We pulled up in front of Kiyuki's house, and then I shot her a text to say that we were here. After a couple minutes, she came outside wearing a tight red number. Her long dark hair was in a ponytail, and her vanilla complexion was flawless.

"Hey pretties," she beamed and slid into the backseat of the car.

"Hello, you look sexy. I'm surprised Deshawn let you out looking like that," I taunted.

"He almost didn't. You see his ass watching from the window like he's my damn daddy," Kiyuki laughed and so did we.

"They say if a man isn't jealous, then that's a bad sign," I said.

"What is up with you and all these damn quotes?" Namiko frowned as she pulled away from the curb.

"I've been reading this relationship book," I chuckled.

We talked for the rest of the ride, and enjoyed the Young Thug mixtape the whole way to Joe Muer's. It wasn't busy when we walked in, so we were seated immediately. After we placed our drink and food orders, we were left there to converse with one another.

"So how are you feeling Aniku?" Kiyuki questioned and sipped her water.

"I'm regular, why?" I frowned. She and Namiko gave one another a look, and then directed their attention back to me.

"Well you're pregnant and in school, so I was wondering how everything was going? You can't possibly feel regular," Kiyuki frowned in confusion.

"Well I do," I shrugged.

"I don't think you fully understand what is about to happen with your life," Namiko chimed in and stared at me.

"I do get it. I just have it all planned out," I nodded. "You're still in school Namiko, and *you* have a baby," I reminded her.

"You're right, but I'm married and my baby was intentional. Maximilian and I literally made Baby Max on purpose," she replied.

"And what is this plan you have?" Kiyuki quizzed.

"Your baby wasn't even planned Kiyuki, so don't start!" I put my hand up signaling a stop sign.

"It sure wasn't Aniku, but I wasn't floating around Michigan like everything was okay. Shit half of my pregnancy I was miserable and broke," she spat.

"Well that won't be me," I assured them.

"What is this plan Aniku?" Namiko repeated Kiyuki's question.

"While I'm in class and doing homework, Konz will take care of the baby. If I have a big paper or study session, he will care for the baby then too," I smiled.

"And what if Konz has to work? You know he doesn't do that gambling shit anymore, he works for Max now," Kiyuki said.

"I will just have you guys babysit," I chuckled.

"I don't mind helping you Aniku, but you need to understand that it won't be like the TV shows or movies," Kiyuki responded sternly.

"Why does it matter to y'all anyway? It's my baby," I pouted.

"It matters because we love you, and you may not want to hear this, but you're still a baby your damn self," Namiko furrowed her brows.

"I'm not a baby," was all I could say in response.

"You know what I mean. You need to grow up Aniku, and very quickly. Being a mom is not something you can turn on and turn off. You can't have your regular life and then say, okay I'm ready to be a mom for the rest of the day," Namiko added.

"So what are y'all saying? Get an abortion?" I raised a brow.

"We're not telling you to do anything. It's your body. We're just trying to make sure that you're preparing yourself, and that you understand how serious it is being a mother. Once that baby gets here, your life is not your own anymore. At least not until they're about twenty-five," Kiyuki smiled at me.

"I'm gonna get it together, I promise," I half smiled and so did they.

Just then, our food arrived. For the rest of the night we talked about how I would handle becoming a mother. I was slightly annoyed, but I knew they were right. I really needed to shape up. I would die before I proved my sisters and Konz right about not being ready. I wasn't a child when I laid down and made the baby, so it wasn't the time for me to act like one now. One thing that I did enjoy about their lecture was the fact that it felt like old times again.

DESHAWN

"I can't believe y'all have never been here," I chuckled and took a swig of my beer. Maximilian, my little brother Robbie, and I were chilling at Purple Fire watching some of the dancers.

"I don't really come to strip clubs like that. I be too busy," Max smiled. Robbie mugged him, so I smacked his arm.

Now that everybody was making up, and shit, I was attempting to get my brother and best friend to be cordial at least. To be honest, I didn't quite understand the beef they had with each other. On top of that, it seemed that Robbie was the main one with the problem, and Max just didn't like Robbie because he didn't like him.

"Well you need to get out more," I replied to Max.

"Sorry, I would rather make money than spend it. But do you," he smirked.

"This nigga," Robbie mumbled and smacked his lips.

"A'ight what's up? That's the last time I'm gone let your little bitch ass side remarks and noises slide," Max shot up out of his seat.

"Aye chill!" I shouted.

"What the fuck you gon' do nigga? Everybody else may be fearful of you, but not me!" Robbie yelled and stood up as well.

"You ain't said nothing but a word, let's go outside muthafucka,"

Max smiled and raced out of the club with Robbie right on his heels. This shit was not going as planned.

I ran outside after them, and as soon as both of their feet hit the pavement, they started to go at it. Robbie swung and missed, causing him to lose his balance, so Max punched his ass in the stomach. Then Max delivered another blow to his nose, mouth, and then his chin.

"Stop y'all! What the fuck! Y'all out here fighting like some fuckin hoodlums!" I hollered and tried to intervene.

Robbie appeared to be a little dazed from the punches that Max had thrown his way, but he wasn't ready to tap out. Max was shooting daggers at him, just waiting for him to try and swing again. As he wished, Robbie swung and the punch landed on Max's neck. *C'mon little bro, you can do better than that*, I thought and shook my head. I pulled on Max, but he roughly moved from my embrace, wanting to continue the battle. He then gave Robbie a quick two-piece, landing on his nose and between the eyes. Robbie fell backwards, and slumped onto the ground.

"Arrggh," he groaned in pain.

"Come on little nigga. You been barking all this shit for months, let's go," Max cheered Robbie on. Robbie just glared at him as I tried to help him stand up.

"Y'all need to cut this shit out!" I shouted.

"You talk to your fucking brother. He the one that has a fucking problem with me for no damn reason," Max panted.

"Because unlike this nigga, I don't appreciate the way you did my damn sister," Robbie screamed as innocent bystanders looked on.

"Negro please, get the fuck over it. Your sister knew what was up from the damn jump! She's a grown ass woman, and if she chose to fuck with me knowing it wasn't gone be nothing then that's on her!" Max responded angrily. He was right though, no matter what I said, Cori was gonna fuck with Max regardless.

"You can't be mad at him over Cori nigga. She wanted to be with Max, even though she knew it wasn't going anywhere," I frowned down at Robbie.

"You should've just stopped talking to her," Robbie barked.

"I have, on many occasions. Ain't nobody saying it's all Cori's fault.

All I'm saying is that you can't be mad at me. Your sister was fucking with me willingly Robbie," Max replied.

"This shit ain't worth it bro. It's way bigger shit going on, and you wanna have beef over this?" I looked at Robbie confused. "It's niggas out here dying and getting robbed every day, and you trying to start wars over a relationship that your grown sister participated in?"

"I love my sister man. I don't know about you," Robbie glared at me.

"You don't know about me?" I chuckled. "If I didn't love Cori she would've been dead the day she stepped off that fucking plane!" I shouted.

"Nah, she would've been dead before she even left nigga. If it wasn't for Deshawn, I would've been killed Cori's ass," Max added.

"What's going on with you man? This can't be all over Cori and Max's relationship," I kneeled down beside him. Robbie just looked away, with his face still twisted up. "Talk man, this is the time to get all this shit out," I said.

He looked up at Maximilian, looked away, and then looked back up at him. "Why you ain't never put me on the team?" he scowled.

"That's what this is over?" Max jerked his neck back surprised.

"Yeah man, we all grew up together, you, me, Deshawn, and Konz, yet you never once let me get down with y'all. Konz had the choice but declined, and you still didn't even ask me. I thought we were all like brothers, but I guess not," he huffed.

"Robbie man, I ain't even know that you wanted to be down with us. I don't even ask people to be down; people come to me. The only reason I asked Konz was because I was seeing firsthand how he had absolutely no income," Max shrugged.

"Robbie you know all four of us are like brothers. We grew up that way and it's still that way. Him not asking you to be on the team was nothing personal," I added.

Robbie took a deep breath before speaking, "Aye, umm, I'm sorry. I guess I should've just spoken up instead of trying to have beef with you," he pursed his lips.

"You right and I should've tried to sit you down and talk, instead of just brushing it off," Max smiled and so did Robbie.

"So y'all good?" I grinned and looked back and forth between the two.

"Are we?" Max cheesed.

Robbie twisted his mouth up before saying, "Yeah we good, but it's gone take some time for me to forgive you for fucking my grill up," he joked and we all chuckled.

"Well if it's any consolation, why don't you come by office on Wednesday and we can discuss putting you to work," Max replied.

"I think that would make me feel a little better. And you can buy me a drink," Robbie said and then turned to go back inside the strip club.

"Aye what about your face nigga?" I frowned.

"Splash some water on my shit, it'll be good. Plus, these bitches only care about how much money you throwing, not if you got a busted nose or not," he said over his shoulder and continued walking in.

Max and I shook our heads, and then followed him. I was just happy that we could all go back to being cool again.

Shit was really starting to look up. I had the woman I loved, a beautiful daughter, and my brother and best friend were back to being like family. God was good.

MAXIMILIAN

Today was a long ass day, and before I went home, I wanted to stop and have a drink. I just wanted some alone time so that I could clear my head. Not that anything was wrong, but I just liked to take time to myself and do a little mental hygiene.

My bar of choice was Starter's on Woodward Avenue. It was attached to an apartment building, and I always came here when I lived alone. It reminded me of the times when I was carefree and just living life. I liked to come here whenever I needed a little reset, because those memories would always help me relax.

"What you doing in my building?" I heard a familiar voice say. I looked over my shoulder after polishing off my Jack, and saw that nurse Melissa.

"Oh what's up? I ain't know you lived here," I half smiled and then turned around to let the bartender know I wanted more.

"Sure you didn't," she chuckled and sat next to me. "So we haven't talked in a while," she smiled and then ordered a drink.

"I know," I shrugged.

"Where have you been? For a minute I thought you ran off after I gave you the goodies," laughed.

"I didn't run off, I just got my shit back together," I replied and took a sip of my drink.

"You seemed to always have it together in my eyes. Except for a few minor details," she grinned.

"Oh yeah, like what?" I raised a brow as if I was interested in this conversation.

"Your choice in women of course. I think I suit you better, and so does your mom. Speaking of your mom, how is she?" she asked.

"She's moved on to greener pastures." I responded dryly. I didn't feel the need to get into details with this girl. She was irritating me anyway.

"Oh, I liked her. She liked me for you. You know that right?"

"My mom was always known for being wrong," I smiled at her and she smacked her lips at me.

"Whatever. So when can we hang out again?" she sipped her martini.

"Melissa, come on man. I'm gonna be honest with you. I was dealing with some shit and that's why we ended up in bed together, but I'm not trying to deal with you on that level. I wanna apologize though, if you feel like I used you."

"An apology isn't gonna really help me," she laughed wryly.

"I shouldn't have fucked you, but look, I won't even tell anybody. We can act like we never even met," I grinned.

"What? No!" she squealed. "I'm not that upset, but I just wish that I had met you before you got married I guess," she shrugged and played with her martini straw.

"Well everything happens for a reason. My wife and I were meant to be."

"Why do you say that? How can you even be so sure?" she frowned.

"Because I've never felt the way I feel when I'm with her. And she got me to marry her so that's something within itself," I chuckled.

"Yeah, I guess that's true," she pursed her lips. "But, if you didn't know her and she wasn't your wife, would you have given us a real shot?" she smirked.

"I don't know, you kind of crazy," I half joked and she laughed.

"Crazy how?" she cocked her head.

"The way you're always wherever I'm at, that's kind of weird shorty," I squinted my eyes in a suspicious manner.

"I swear to God it's a coincidence Max," she cackled. "Every time I go somewhere, it seems that you're always there. But like you said, everything happens for a reason. Maybe God keeps putting you in my path for a reason," she bit her lip.

"Yeah, to show you what you will never have," I laughed.

"Ah! You're such an asshole Max," she cheesed. "I like it though, a lot," she half smiled. "You think that we can at least be friends?"

"That is probably not the best idea. Do you honestly think my wife will want you over for Christmas dinner knowing she saw you floating around my loft half naked?"

"She probably wouldn't. Maybe I can just be someone to talk to when you can't talk to anyone else?" she offered and I shook my head. "No? Okay," she chuckled.

"If I see you out, I'm gone always say what's up and speak to you. We don't need to be texting and calling each other, or meeting for lunch though. Let's just be cordial," I pinched her chin and she blushed.

"That's cool."

"And if you need me to knock somebody out for you, I can do that too," I joked.

"I'll be sure to send a pigeon with my message if I need that service," she laughed.

"You do that," I winked.

I talked with Melissa for about half an hour longer, and then decided to head home. I walked inside, and I heard my son's laughs and coos. I followed the sound, and ended up in his playroom where I saw Namiko, Baby Max, and Dorothea playing with Baby Max's toys.

"What y'all doing?" I smiled and walked in.

"There's daddy!" Namiko smiled down at our son with her pretty ass. "Say hi daddy," she kissed his cheek.

"Hey sexy," I kissed Namiko's lips and then sat down to play with them as well.

"I will go start dinner," Dorothea smiled and tapped my shoulder. Before she left, she took a couple pictures of us as a family.

NAMIKO

Chris Brown's "Make Love" spilled through the speakers as I lit the candles on the dinner table. I smoothed down the little teddy I had on, and then straightened the silverware I'd set out.

I heard the front door slam from far away, and I knew Maximilian was here. I knew he would follow the sound of the music, and end up right where I wanted him. I fumbled over the pose I wanted to be in when he arrived. I decided just to sit on the edge of the table, and slightly cross my legs. As soon as I did so, he appeared in the doorway of the dining room.

"Look at you," he bit his lip and started towards me.

"Wait Max, sit down," I giggled and nudged his horny ass off me. He sat down in the chair, and when I tried to walk to my side, he yanked me down into his lap.

"We can eat out of the same plate, I'm not that hungry; at least not for this," he planted kisses up my arm.

"I'm really hungry Max," I whined as he kissed on my neck gently. My pussy was starting to get wet, and I knew in a minute I wouldn't be in any mood to talk.

"Eat. I'm just kissing you," he mumbled and continued to peck all over my neck and collarbone. "Back to Sleep" by Chris Brown came on, putting me more in the mood. I knew I needed to get it out now, or it would never happen tonight.

"Max, I'm pregnant," I blurted out. He stopped kissing my neck, pulled back, and looked up into my eyes.

"You look even more beautiful now," he whispered. I half smiled and then planted a kiss on his lips. "Hurry up and eat so that I can take you upstairs and eat," he added.

I took a few bites of the macaroni and cheese, but before I could take another bite of the chicken, he picked me up to take me upstairs. He laid me on the bed, and then pulled my teddy over my head. He immediately began to devour my nipples, while playing with my wet center.

"Aahh," I purred.

He climbed off me, and then undressed down to his birthday suit. He got back on the bed, and positioned himself in between my legs. He pressed his lips against mine gently, and kissed me passionately. It felt so good that I could kiss him like that forever. He then started to kiss me harder, making me even wetter.

"I love you Nami," he said in a low tone.

I felt the head of his dick at my opening, and then he began to push himself inside me. I bit down on my lip as we stared each other's in the eyes. He moved slowly in and out of me, and I felt like I would cum any minute.

"Ahhh Max," I whimpered in between kisses.

With every pump, I could feel slight pain but plenty of pleasure. I ran my hands up and down his muscular back, as he continued to hit my spot.

"Ugghh," I groaned softly as I gushed on his rod.

"Damn," he moaned and then trailed kisses from my lips to my neck. His big hands caressed my thighs and groped my breasts roughly, yet gently.

"I love you more Max," I cooed right before he began to tongue me down.

NAMIKO DAVIS

TWO YEARS LATER ... NEW YEAR'S EVE NIGHT...

It was New Year's Eve, and everybody was here at Max's and my home. Kiyuki was here, as well as Deshawn, with their daughter Mai and son Deshawn Jr. Deshawn Jr. or DJ was so cute, and looked exactly like his father. Kiyuki and Deshawn were married now, and they were picture perfect. I have never seen my sister this happy, and it made me happy to see her this way. As promised, our relationship only got better over time. It felt so good to have my older sister back.

My baby sister Aniku was here as well with Konz, and surprisingly they were great parents to a little boy they named Aakil. They were gonna name him after Konz, but Konz hates his name and refused. I was really worried about my sister becoming a mother, but she proved us all wrong. She was balancing life and motherhood extremely well. She had a few mishaps here and there, but nothing too serious.

"Namiko where is the champagne?" Cori asked me.

"It's in the last cabinet on the left," I smiled and continued to wipe mustard off Maximilian Jr.'s face.

Yes, Cori and I were cordial now. She got over the fact that she couldn't be with Max, and over time, we became cool. She was even okay with Kiyuki. They weren't best friends, neither were she and I, but we would all hang out sometimes, which was good. I preferred it that way, because I didn't like having problems with people, no matter who they were. I still kept my eye on her every now and then though.

"Okay, okay," Max Jr. whined referring to me wiping his mouth. "I'm clean now mommy," he pouted with his cute self.

"Okay go," I stood up and let him run out. He was the most grown three-year-old I'd ever run across.

I walked out of the bathroom, and headed down the hall to get my two-year-old daughter, Naori. I grabbed her out of her playpen, and then headed back out to the den where the party was. Naori looked just like Max and I mixed, and she was the cutest with her dark caramel complexion. I kissed her cheek as I entered the den. I spotted Maximilian with MJ, and so I sat down next to him.

"I didn't think you were gonna be back in time for the New Year's kiss," Max joked and smiled with his sexy ass.

"I wouldn't miss any chance to kiss you," I winked and he kissed my neck lightly.

As for me, I was finally done with college at Wayne State, and now in the process of getting my Master's Degree. When I was done, I would finally be able to get a job as a Forensic Anthropologist. I was hoping to be hired by the FBI soon, because they paid more, but I knew that took time. I was willing to work hard for it though.

"Thank you," I said to Kiyuki as she went around the room handing out champagne glasses.

"Apple cider for you," she smiled down at Evelyn. Evelyn was now pregnant by her boyfriend of two years named Robert. I was so excited as if it was my baby when she told me. I loved her and Robert together, because he really treated my best friend the way she deserved.

I smiled at she and Kiyuki's quick interaction, because I was happy to see that they'd become cool. I loved that everyone could be mature and act like adults. All the scheming, lying, fighting, and backstabbing was way behind us and it felt good.

"Okay, its countdown time y'all!" Robbie shouted to the room, and everyone got situated.

"Alright, 10, 9, 8, 7, 6, 5, 4, 3, 2, 1, Happy New Year!" we all shouted and all the couples kissed.

"To another great year, and plenty more beautiful," Max said in a low tone.

"Cheers to that handsome," I giggled and we clinked our glasses together.

*FIN*

Become a VIP Reader!

*To join my mailing list text **SHVONNE** to **66866** and stay up to date! Also, join **Shvonne Latrice Reading Group** on Facebook!*